Degas in New Orleans

by Rosary Hartel O'Neill

A SAMUEL FRENCH ACTING EDITION

SAMUEL
FRENCH

FOUNDED 1830

NEW YORK HOLLYWOOD LONDON TORONTO

SAMUELFRENCH.COM

ISBN 978-0-573-69762-3   Printed in U.S.A.   #6255

MUSIC USE NOTE

**IMPORTANT BILLING AND CREDIT
REQUIREMENTS**

CHARACTERS

EDGAR DEGAS – 38, the famous painter

RENÉ DEGAS – 27, Edgar's brother

ESTELLE (TELL) MUSSON BALFOUR DEGAS – 29, René's wife

DESIREE (DIDI) MUSSON – 34, Tell's sister

MATHILDE MUSSON BELL – 31, Tell's sister

MICHEL MUSSON – 60, Tell's father

JOSEPHINE (JO) BALFOUR – 10, Tell's daughter

AMERICA DURRIVE OLIVIER – 24, a neighbor

EMILY CUCKOW RILLIEUX – 45, a cousin, of mixed race, brown skin

MAN #1 – Will Bell— husband of Mathilde, funeral collector, soldier

MAN #2 – Mendicant, servant, soldier

ACCENTS

Family members speak with a soft, gentle, urbane upper-class New Orleans accent. America has a harsher, nasal, lower class drawl. Edgar speaks English with a pronounced accent. René who has lived in New Orleans for six years has lost most of his accent.

SETTING

We are in a two-story rental house on 2306 Esplanade Avenue, New Orleans, Louisiana. It is 1872. A double parlor with the remnants of grandeur: a glittering chandelier, an elegant tattered sofa, a mahogany desk, and a high-back chair. To the right, two floor-to-ceiling windows open onto a galley; to the left, a door to the pantry. Upstage two matching parlor doors lead offstage to an unseen staircased grand hallway that connects the upstairs, and the front and rear of the house. Outside we hear the clanging of a random mule-drawn streetcar. One possibility, throughout the play is to have Degas' paintings or the rapturous colors within them projected onto the rear wall, enriching the bleak setting with their transparent blues, pinks, and violets.

DEGAS IN NEW ORLEANS was first performed in June 2002 in New Orleans.

PROLOGUE

*(**SOUND**: Music playing softly)*

*(**EDGAR** stands outside the house on Esplanade at an easel painting. As he mentions his cousins and brother they enter and pose in a tableau of beautiful young people)*

EDGAR. I have a picture in my mind of the best painting I never painted: three women and two men in untouched expectation. It's October, 1872. I've come to New Orleans to find myself as a painter and close this hole in my soul. My brother René is there, the bloom of youth on his cheek. We're dining at our uncle's, our enthusiasm buoyed by the lightness of each other. My cousins are there, Didi and Mathilde. And Tell, beautiful Tell, a Civil War widow and already remarried. First time I've seen the girls since they rode out the Civil War with us in France. And oh, the sunlight and the, God knows why, laughter. We are young and dreams seem possible *(Music fades out)*

(Slides—Degas' face and then the Degas house on Esplanade Avenue in New Orleans. Throughout the play we hear music like the compositions of Erik Satie.)

(blackout)

ACT ONE

Scene One

(October 25, 1872–5:30 a.m. Satie music and slides of the Degas House at the same time)

JO BALFOUR, 10, is asleep on the floor, in a pink tutu and ballet slippers, her hair caught in a ribboned ponytail like Degas' statue of La Fille de Quatorze Ans. JO rises dreamily and begins to dance. She lies back on the floor, returning to her sleeping state.)

(SOUND: Music fades, slides out, lights up)

(TELL DEGAS, 29, crosses the stage. She is exquisite, fragile with a porcelain beauty. Now and then she pauses to stabilize herself. She trips on her daughter's legs, and cries distraught)

TELL. Jo, You're supposed to sleep on the sofa.

JO. *(Gets up restlessly)* Oh Mommy. I dreamed I was a bird and could fly high, but I flew into a clothesline —

TELL. Fold up your sheets.

JO. Why do I have to give my room to Uncle Edgar?

TELL. Are you listening to me?

JO. I want Uncle to paint you, Mama. You're so beautiful. If he would have painted Papa, he'd have been with me always. I don't know what he looked like. If Uncle paints you, you'll be with me forever.

(TELL smiles, puts an arm around JO's shoulder—coaxingly)

TELL. Get dressed—

(A burst of laughter comes from the hallway. JO hurries out, and TELL slips out. We see a pantomime of activity occurring in the house as the family awakens and prepares for EDGAR.)

(MATHILDE, 31, an elegant but frazzled woman, walks in through the pantry with a tray with a coffee pot and cups and saucers. Pours her coffee expectantly and sits on the sofa. **UNCLE MICHEL**, *60, dressed in a Confederate Army uniform, barges in from the front hallway followed by* **DIDI**, *34, an intense pretty lady with soft features. All move quickly, full of eager anticipation to greet* **EDGAR** *first.)*

UNCLE MICHEL. No matter how early I get up, it's never early enough. *(Goes to the back parlor doorway and calls)* Out, Jo, out.

DIDI. *(Shocked but giggling)* Shush, Papa. Take off that uniform. Someone's going to shoot you.

UNCLE MICHEL. I need to greet my nephew in style.

MATHILDE. *(Pats his shoulder playfully)* Go back to sleep, Papa.

UNCLE MICHEL. I just want to have a quiet cup of coffee alone.

DIDI. I just wanted to have a quiet cup of coffee alone.

UNCLE MICHEL. *(Indignantly)* Jo, out. *(Grumbling)* The dressing room is always occupied in this house. God, I've got a headache.

JO. *(From the rear hallway shouts)* One minute.

MATHILDE. *(With a warning look)* You should stop drinking.

UNCLE MICHEL. Babies screaming through the night.

DIDI. Put some sherry on their lips.

UNCLE MICHEL. Or let me kill one of them. *(Calls toward the back parlor doorway)* Jo. Get out. *(Shrugging his shoulders)* Mathilde, I want you to help Didi fix up. Didi needs a husband. Edgar is her last chance. A girl's life is like a ship. When she's sixteen, you've got to launch her, deck her with flags and ribbons, sail her out. At twenty-three, the ship turns and starts back to port. Didi is at the dock.

MATHILDE. Good morning to you too.

UNCLE MICHEL. *(To* **DIDI***)* Who's going to care for you when I keel over? Your sisters' husbands? The church? Remember what your mother said about those spinsters, who spied on their married neighbor. They'd snicker when they

7

heard her husband beating her or when they saw bruises on her arm. One day, that wife charged out of her house and screamed, "You can laugh and you can hiss but on me tombstone won't be, 'Miss.'"

MATHILDE. Just let us enjoy Edgar's company as we did in Paris.

UNCLE MICHEL. Keep away from Edgar. You've got a husband.

JO. *(Shouts from the dressing room)* Finished.

UNCLE MICHEL. Excuse me, girls. *(He leans over, kisses* **DIDI'***s cheek, then adds with a constrained air)* Mathilde, do Didi's hair like yours. She looks like a gargoyle.

*(***UNCLE MICHEL** *exits.)*

(Seconds later, in the hallway, **RENÉ** *tosses back his dark hair as* **TELL** *goes to embrace him. Gorgeous, he wears a single-breasted coat reaching mid-thigh over his white night shirt.)*

RENÉ. Did you already spoil your dress?

TELL. I stumbled—*(Pause)* Have you seen the children?

RENÉ. Yes, but they're asking for you. Mind them inside. I don't want to see grass stains on their outfits. Your son's knickers are already split...I'm sleeping till noon. Don't let the babies wake me. *(He turns to go, rubbing his sweaty forehead.)* Sorry about last night. The trip back from Paris was rough.

TELL. You fell right to sleep. I hoped to...–

RENÉ. I can't seem to get romantic when first thing I spot is bills on my dresser. Didn't you pay a thing while I was gone!

TELL. With what?

RENÉ. Maybe I'm exhausted from the overseas crossing. *(He gives her a cold peck.)* You're the center of my universe. I dote on you like the sun rising.

*(***RENÉ** *slouches off. A horn from a lone ship howls in the distance.* **TELL** *enters the parlor.)*

TELL. Sorry I couldn't go up to the station. How did you find Edgar?

MATHILDE. Last night? *(She chuckles—then with a pleased, relieved air)* He seemed uncertain, tentative, as if he had some secret. He was all dressed the part of the painter/poet—so kind and so subdued. You know how bachelors do.

TELL. It's sad. They're not going to get drawn into matrimony, but they practice in case the real thing—

(From the hallway, **JO** *and* **UNCLE MICHEL** *'s voices are heard)*

DIDI. *(Hastily)* Have you told René about the new item?

TELL. *(Too vehemently)* Not yet. Don't say anything. Y'all promised.

*(***UNCLE MICHEL** *and* **JO** *dash in, enthusiastically fencing with canes.)*

JO. Mommy.

TELL. Stop, Jo.

DIDI. It's not her, it's him.

UNCLE MICHEL. Move back the furniture.

DIDI. *(Resentful)* It's not my turn to watch him.

*(***UNCLE MICHEL** *and* **JO** *go out into the front hallway, still fencing.* **DIDI** *and* **TELL** *follow. She turns back irritated.)*

TELL. Yes, but if the furniture is off—

MATHILDE. By an inch, I know.

*(***DIDI** *hurries* **TELL** *off through the back parlor doorway.* **MATHILDE** *gets some coffee, looks out the gallery window and spots* **EDGAR.***)*

MATHILDE. Edgar? Oh Lord. Come on in. There you are—*(Calls out)* Everybody! Edgar is up!

*(***EDGAR** *pokes through a gallery window. She stops abruptly, overcome by acute self-consciousness.)*

MATHILDE. Why are you looking at me like that? I know I've changed.

EDGAR. *(With awkward tenderness)* You look wonderful as I told you last night. *(Drawn to a picture)* Is this Tell's wedding portrait?

MATHILDE. To Joe Balfour. She was sixteen.

EDGAR. She looks like a pouty child.

MATHILDE. Not with those breasts. She got the family collection.

(UNCLE MICHEL's and JO's voices are heard in the hallway. They enter in a flurry)

UNCLE MICHEL. There you are. Welcome, Edgar.

EDGAR. *(Takes her hands and gently lifts them up)* Can't be Jo. Such a big girl.

JO. Will you stay with us forever—

(DIDI comes in from the back parlor)

DIDI. You're up already.

EDGAR. You've a different hair-do.

DIDI. You noticed.

(She smiles and hugs him gratefully. He turns, sees TELL standing quietly in the front parlor doorway.)

EDGAR. Tell, is that you? You're even more beautiful than when I—

TELL. *(Embarrassed and pleased)* Hello, Edgar.

EDGAR. *(Catches himself)* All the Musson sisters...beautiful.

(DIDI, MATHILDE, and JO surround EDGAR. UNCLE MICHEL salutes him.)

ALL GIRLS TOGETHER. *(To EDGAR)* Paint me. And the children. A family group!

DIDI. It doesn't matter what you draw. Friends think you're great, soon as they know you studied paintings at the Louvre.

EDGAR. I'm hoping I'll paint best here. I love your big trees that throw their arms before the sky, your flowers that change colors— Audubon went to Barataria—I'll claim Louisiana. Stake out the galleries, the pillars, the shade. I want to find a new spatiality in my drawings ... I have always been ambitious. Too much so. *(Looking at* **TELL***)* Family, beware. I don't know where I'll settle down, near you probably, but I'm not going to live near a park with nurses and swings.

UNCLE MICHEL. Yes, Didi is the one who knows about art. *(Rings a bell and screams)* You can clear now.

COOKS. *(offstage)* "We ain't no slaves."

DIDI. *(Self-righteously)* It's fine; I'll get it.

*(***MATHILDE** *makes a great business of stacking the cups, and gathering napkins.* **DIDI** *bangs silver.)*

UNCLE MICHEL. The family want to know what Edgar is really going to do in New Orleans—

EDGAR. To paint!

UNCLE MICHEL. *(Jolting back)* Excuse me. Some of us have to work! Let's leave Didi with Edgar.

TELL. Fine.

(With a knowing nod to **DIDI**, **UNCLE MICHEL**, **MATHILDE**, **JO**, *slip out. But* **EDGAR** *takes* **TELL** *by the hand, leaves* **DIDI** *and scoots* **TELL** *to the gallery.)*

TELL. What are you doing?

EDGAR. I paint by intuition. I have to capture you, before the lights fade.

TELL. That's not what Papa and my brother-in-law have —

EDGAR. What does Will do?

TELL. He ... He used to sell materials for bagging cotton.

(SOUND: Street cries. Peddlers hawk their wares, a horn strains from a ship on the Mississippi. **EDGAR** *backs against the column lit by the sun and paints)*

*(*WILL*, a short stocky man bursts through the door, walking with a stiff wobble. A flask peeks out of his pocket. He hurries over to* **EDGAR***.)*

WILL. I'm late for a meeting. But when I get back, I want to talk you.

*(*WILL *shakes* **EDGAR***'s hand three times, wipes his palm against his jacket, and stumbles off.)*

TELL. Stay away from him as long as you can.

(Their eyes pause on each other. Inside, trays bang about.)

TELL. *(Quickly)* We do our own cooking now—They say you arrived in the wee hours... where have you been?

EDGAR. Outside, drawing. Taking the winter blues off the land, up with the sun. *(He picks up his paints and sketchpad awkwardly, unable to look at her.)* Smelling the magnolias and honeysuckle—I'm here to *(Pause)* find a new approach to my painting. *(Pause)* But the ground is so untamed.

TELL. *(Clearing her throat)* The servants refuse to do yard work.

(He wipes off a dewy chair, seats her.)

EDGAR. You wouldn't believe how my brother went on about the landscapes I could paint. But the streets look so unsettled.

TELL. Why not paint on the gallery. We can protect one place from children.

(SOUND: "Oh, no, no, no!" A woman wails next door.)

TELL. Doctors have fled; men starve in the streets... *(Another wail pierces the air)* There's always a child in a sick room...But...you're resilient.

*(*EDGAR *keeps looking at her as if waiting for something more.)*

TELL. Did you expect the city to be different? Why are you staring?

EDGAR. You're still the beauty. *(Pause)* René wants me to paint Jackson Square *(Pause)* the Mississippi *(Pause)* the Cotton Exchange.

TELL. Be sure you... avoid the back streets.

(Sounds of children burst from the house. **EDGAR** *and* **TELL** *shrink back, while her sisters walk outside and empty their own slops into the gutter.)*

TELL. Didn't René tell you we have to do everything? The plantation was leveled.

EDGAR. And your in-town home—

TELL. Lost to taxes. You can't read the lists of the dead in the paper; there are so many pages.

(From inside a woman screams. "I'm not doing the wash again.")

TELL. I'm glad Mama died before we moved.

*(**SOUND:** Inside the house, a woman shrieks and a child whines.)*

TELL. My sisters! One cares for rowdy kids. The other tends to Papa.

*(**SOUND:** The clanking of pots and cutlery soars from the kitchen, and the bustle of children.)*

EDGAR. How many of your family live here?

TELL. Eighteen plus a few servants. . .

EDGAR. I should leave.

(Lamps are turned up, brooms rush over the floors.)

TELL. *(Confrontational)* No! After such a long journey! Everyone is counting on you.

EDGAR. Father financed my trip to paint to find new opportunities—

TELL. But you're successful in Paris.

13

EDGAR. On a slow incline. At my last gallery opening, which I myself financed, announcements, caviar, champagne, one thousand hungry people showed up and no one bought a painting. Critics called my work "derivative." I quote, "With this exhibition, Degas has sent his death knell throughout Paris."

TELL. How do you recover from—?

EDGAR. I don't paint for a while. *(He shrugs, returns to painting)* It's hard to extract the arrows alone. Now, when I was with you in France—

TELL. "Our Raphael." That's what we called you.

EDGAR. One Raphael even in a thousand years is enough.

TELL. I'll help you.

EDGAR. How?

TELL. By sparing you too much bad news. By fending off relatives. *(He looks at* **TELL** *with shining eyes; as if she possesses an energy and vitality he needs.)*

EDGAR. You wouldn't advise me to leave painting and have a family?

TELL. Never!

*(***DIDI** *pokes her head out, speaks quickly, unable to tame her excitement)*

DIDI. It's my turn with Edgar.

*(***TELL** *starts to go.)*

EDGAR. Wait. I can keep painting while Didi talks.

*(***TELL** *sits back down and he continues painting.)*

DIDI. *(Pacing, annoyed)* I made a list of things we can discuss. I jotted down novels you might like, and borrowed those I could. We can't always get the latest books, it's not Paris. But I did find *Madame Bovary*, some Dumas *père* and Baudelaire.

EDGAR. I haven't read poetry for a long time.

DIDI. I got Alfred de Musset and George Sand. Are you following... the controversy about her novel, *She and He?*

EDGAR. Not yet.

(He smiles, and **TELL** *smiles back. Then* **DIDI** *changes to a brisk, businesslike air)*

DIDI. The principal figures are artists... I suppose you've read the *Son of Titian?*

EDGAR. Are you still reading a book a week?

DIDI. I do more. I'm writing a novel. Now whenever you paint, I'll work on it.

EDGAR. *(Hesitates, to* **TELL***)* And how are you, Tell?

DIDI. *(To* **EDGAR***)* Fine. Why shouldn't she be? *(Her hands flutter up to her hair)* Did you get my letters? You didn't respond much.

EDGAR. *(Evasively, painting* **TELL***)* Most painters aren't good with words. That is why we draw pictures.

DIDI. I don't like people who talk all the time but say nothing. I like your new signature. One word like Delacroix, not De la Croix. "Degas," not the two words "de Gas" that implies aristocracy. Your brothers were furious. They paid for that false coat of arms. They don't want people to know the family goes back to a bunch of bakers. What I admire most about you is your awareness of the smallest element of art, even one so peripheral and personal as the signature. I've studied the signature and there are similarities between the D in Daumier, the e in Delacroix and the final S in Ingres. I need to find a distinctive professional signature for my writing and a male name like George Sand. With a woman's name you can't become successful. Don't you agree?

EDGAR. Sorry. I wouldn't know.

(He stiffens, looks at her awkwardly, but she flounders on)

DIDI. I amuse myself with letter writing. I used to so look forward to sealing that envelope, placing a stamp. Some I rewrote four or five times to get them perfect. Want to see? *(Takes out letters)* These are the ones I never sent. Next to the ones I received. Silly, but I like to reread them both. My way of being in Paris with you. *(Pause)* I love your stationery and bright blue ink. The paper is so smooth and every letter signed boldly. "Degas." Just like your paintings. I've a special folder for each letter.

(EDGAR is lost in his painting. Rebuffed and hurt, **DIDI** *minces toward the door, peers back)*

DIDI. Edgar I insist you talk to me. Tell, come inside!

(Embarrassed, **EDGAR** *puts down his brush and follows* **DIDI** *inside.* **TELL** *is alone.)*

TELL. Edgar? Edgar. *(Worriedly)* Good. He's gone.

*(***TELL*** rises. She is silent, keeping her chin up, she crosses. She bumps into a chair, with a sigh recovers, moves forward.)*

(EDGAR enters. His expression becomes somber as he stares at her with a growing dread. Suddenly she is self-consciously aware that someone is staring fixedly at her.)

TELL. Edgar?

EDGAR. *(Hesitates, then bursts out guiltily)* Tell, what's wrong? Can't you see me?

TELL. I wasn't paying attention.

EDGAR. I've been watching you. *(Concerned, he touches her arm)* I don't know what to say.

TELL. *(Quickly)* Don't say anything. I'm so ashamed. I wanted to fool you completely.

EDGAR. You can't see? God, you can't see.

TELL. I see a little...I had an infection...a year ago-

EDGAR. Go on.

TELL. A few operations—

EDGAR. You don't have to be embarrassed.

16

TELL. I want you to remember me the way I was.

EDGAR. I do. *(Awkward pause where they smile at each other affectionately.)* All those letters—Didi said nothing. Why didn't René tell me? I'd have come.

TELL. I'd have thrown you out...

EDGAR. Perhaps in Paris the specialists can help. But...What can I do?

TELL. Ask me what I need and I'll tell you. If I'm walking towards a chair and you bring it to me, I'll trip.

EDGAR. You see nothing? Nothing at all?

TELL. Just blurs.

EDGAR. How do you cope?

TELL. I get by working with contrasts. Analyzing the whole moving environment.

EDGAR. Is that so?

TELL. Move and I'll find you. *(He hesitates)* Go on.

EDGAR. I can't...I'm so...I just can't imagine...

TELL. Do it for me.

EDGAR. *(Reluctantly, he moves away)* All right. Should I talk?

TELL. *(Laughs, a lilt comes into her voice)* No, that would make it too easy. Go on.

(He moves away; she walks in the wrong direction; he steps into her path)

TELL. There! I found you. *(Changing the subject)* See? Do you look different?

EDGAR. I have a few gray hairs, but they say my shoulders are stronger.

TELL. May I touch your face? *(Her hands glide lovingly over his features. He squeezes her hands)* You haven't changed much. What's this scar?

EDGAR. A ricochet wound. From fighting in the Commune.

17

TELL. Fighting!

EDGAR. I've staggered through blood baths and watched my friends die. Anybody in any way connected to the Commune or in the wrong place was shot.

TELL. But you survived.

EDGAR. Because I was mistaken for a corpse. All the friends I had in Paris are unhappy or dead. I'm here to make a new life in New Orleans. Here let me paint you.

TELL. I'm not as pretty as I was.

EDGAR. You've a gentler, more refined beauty.

NURSE. *(offstage)* Miss Tell. Time for the children's baths.

(EDGAR goes to the doorway and yells)

EDGAR. She's gone for a walk. Start without her.

DIDI. *(Peeking out)* Edgar should visit with Papa over his paper and Tell rock her baby.

EDGAR. Later.

(He moves his easel, and sits **TELL** *in a corner chair. The warm morning sun brightens her face. He unbuttons her collar.)*

EDGAR. Your life is so demanding.

TELL. I don't work harder than you. Tell me what you do each moment.

(He takes off his coat and yanks out his spotted cotton shirt.)

EDGAR. I work with broad strokes. Keeping the design simple—.

(A Negro in a gray wool cavalry shirt, carrying a baby, creeps to the gallery. **EDGAR** *gives him some money and the man retreats.* **TELL** *grasps her chair.)*

TELL. Now, they'll all be begging here.

EDGAR. We can't let them starve.

(EDGAR hands TELL a little fan, his movements awkward as he touches her.)

TELL. *(Fanning herself)* You've no idea how difficult life has been. No progress has been made since the War. I think in Europe you call it the War Between the States. We call it the War against Northern Aggression.

(Mournful sounds drift in from a funeral procession down the street.)

TELL. They parade toward St. Louis Cemetery No. 3, to the tombs of the old Creole families.

(Bells toll from the Saint Louis Cathedral)

EDGAR. My god. A man heading the cortege is coming to the gallery, collecting for the casket. I'll oblige him.

(TELL shudders, wipes her brow. EDGAR gives the man money, returns to his painting.)

TELL. What are you doing now?

(He puts down the brush and steps from the canvas to the railing.)

TELL. What's going on?

EDGAR. Some soldier has left the procession and fallen on a crutch. Is this normal?

TELL. Yes. I guess we've gotten used to it...funerals. Everyone has a brother, father, cousin, husband...

EDGAR. I'm so sorry. *(He comes over, bends down, and repositions her in the chair. He looks away as he speaks.)* Our revolution, the Commune, sprang from the masses, and found its martyrs. . . in the little people. Artists and—

TELL. Is that why you came?

EDGAR. Travel is a more gracious way to bid farewell than sobbing at the scene. Now there will be less in my life—just painting and brave people like you. Most of us can only let go of a little at a time.

19

TELL. Emptiness will create new paths. Paint what you see now!

EDGAR. But no one, even family, wants me to paint.

TELL. We all need art; we take it for granted.

EDGAR. What if I spend 18 hours a day painting while the family starves?

TELL. Shoosh. Once you're successful...your glory will revive our dreams.

EDGAR. But if I fail?

TELL. Paint with a velocity that won't let you.

EDGAR. Whom should I paint?

TELL. The family. Me. Make us important.

EDGAR. If I paint well, there won't be time for anything else—

TELL. Be selfish. Cut people before you cut painting.

(RENÉ shouts from the hall, "Tell! Tell!" She fans her sweaty cheeks.)

TELL. *(Calls out)* I'm here! *(To* **EDGAR***)* Don't leave anything outside, you don't want stolen.

(EDGAR collapses his easel, throws his paints in a box.)

EDGAR. I'll complete your portrait from memory inside.

RENÉ. *(Scowling from the front hallway)* Tell, Tell.

TELL. Up already?

(RENÉ saunters over, enthusiasm covering his hangover)

RENÉ. Morning.

EDGAR. Morning.

(EDGAR exits)

RENÉ. *(Uneasy)* I made a fool of myself, posturing about the wonders of Louisiana, but—

TELL. I have a surprise for you. My heart is racing.

RENÉ. If you're happy that's all that counts.

TELL. I'm so distracted with the thrill of it. I don't want to disappoint you. I'm afraid I'm going to now.

RENÉ. You can't hurt me, Sugar.

TELL. Oh, René, we're going to have a baby.

(RENÉ stops short—then smiles broadly, with a painful effort to be a good sport)

RENÉ. Another child? Oh my God. *(Hugs her, unable to conceal an almost furtive uneasiness)* You said you couldn't get pregnant...A...a third child. We agreed two were enough.

TELL. True, but a baby!

RENÉ. Didn't the doctor forbid this? The other children aren't even three. One a year. Don't you remember how we had to walk the floor! Always some infection, earaches, sore throats, colic.

TELL. You won't have to do anything.

RENÉ. Your father keeps prodding me about making money, about my place as head of the house. I turn around and you're having another baby. Can nothing be done? How did this occur? I thought you were nursing.

TELL. Yes...it's a miracle. God wants this for us, René.

RENÉ. The doctor says you're a high risk. Let's wait to tell the others till you're further along.

(Stung, TELL disappears out the front parlor. He watches her then takes a flask from his pocket and takes a swig. MATHILDE comes through the pantry, her face worried. She is reassured to find RENÉ alone. RENÉ turns, adjusts his jacket.)

MATHILDE. Coffee? It's wonderful to have you home. Did you have a grand time with Edgar in Paris? *(Pause)* I like your new suit.

RENÉ. I've got to give the impression I'm successful, to make money in the future.

MATHILDE. You sound bitter.

RENÉ. That's what I seem like when I'm amused.

MATHILDE. Soon as you settle in we must talk.

RENÉ. Can this wait until later?

*(***UNCLE MICHEL*** and* **JO** *explode through the back parlor door, fencing with canes)*

JO. Parry.

UNCLE MICHEL. Out of my way.

MATHILDE. Papa, please...

*(***UNCLE MICHEL*** and* **JO** *go out the front parlor door.* **RENÉ** *turns on him reproachfully)*

RENÉ. The man doesn't see I'm here. He's my father-in-law.

MATHILDE. You said Edgar would—

RENÉ. *(Yells, in* **UNCLE MICHEL***'s direction)* And he can't say hello. Why is that?

MATHILDE. Is that a yes for—

RENÉ. Yes, but not today... *(She goes to exit with the coffee tray)* Leave the coffee.

MATHILDE. This has to last the week. *(Exits)*

*(**LIGHT:** Focus changes to gallery)*

(RENÉ stares at his flask slinks in a chair, drinks. **EDGAR** *enters, goes to him with a resentful look.)*

EDGAR. She's blind. You couldn't tell me?

RENÉ. *(Floundering)* She swore me to secrecy. She didn't want to see you. And now...

EDGAR. What's wrong?

RENÉ. Tell's...pregnant...I never get sandbagged by men, just women. I've pretty much decided my life is over for the next few years...

EDGAR. Here. *(Unfolding bills from a stack in his pocket)*

RENÉ. That's too much...all right. *(Jovially passes him the flask)* Have some.

EDGAR. So early?

RENÉ. I'm celebrating your arrival New Orleans style. *(Takes another sip)* The thing about Louisiana is nobody's trying to get ahead. You meet amazing people who are not looking for money. They go to parties given by their best friends, that's all. I believe in New Orleans and her possibilities. No place has the flamboyance, the charm this city has. And I don't want us to sell cotton unless selling it makes our lives every day so much richer.

UNCLE MICHEL. *(Comes in from back parlor. He gives a quick suspicious glance from* **RENÉ** *to* **EDGAR***)* Edgar...Welcome. Good you came. I need to talk to you about...Didi.

EDGAR. Why, is something wrong with her?

UNCLE MICHEL. No, no, she is fine. All right, we will talk about her later. *(Solemnly)* First things first...

EDGAR. René is doing well in the cotton business.

UNCLE MICHEL. René is not in the cotton but in the manufacturing business. He manufactures unhappiness.

EDGAR. You are always joking.

UNCLE MICHEL. I won't talk about what it used to be like—when I ran things because that would involve adverse comparisons.

EDGAR. I know René is doing his...

UNCLE MICHEL. The man gives his best energy to traveling and drinking, activities that are clearly not lucrative.

RENÉ. That's not fair.

UNCLE MICHEL. Did you do any business in Paris or did you just have fun?

RENÉ. I negotiated business with my father and I met with Edgar and I spoke to...

UNCLE MICHEL. René used to never say, "I." Then he married Tell...that word became his new toy. He can say, "I want financing for a new venture. I want tickets to Europe. I can't afford another child." Now he pretends he handles things but he runs off or takes a nap.

RENÉ. You misunderstand.

EDGAR. May I help in some way?

UNCLE MICHEL. See if René paid the rent, will you, and any of the bills?

(AMERICA enters. She is a buxom 24 year old beauty, glamorous but overdone, and somewhat loud. Waves a calling card.)

AMERICA. Oh, René, a caller is at the door.

RENÉ. Edgar, may I present Mrs. America Olivier, married to our neighbor, the judge.

AMERICA. My goal is to move to your exotic Paris.

RENÉ. She reads to Tell and helps the children with their music.

EDGAR. How kind.

AMERICA. René wants to move back, too. René, you must warn Edgar about the *gens de colour.* He's got a visitor... *(Hands* **RENÉ** *the calling card.)*...from the wrong side of the blanket.

24

RENÉ. *(Looking at the card)* Cousin Norbert. I hope you're not getting involved with him.

AMERICA. Cousin?

UNCLE MICHEL. *(To AMERICA)* My uncle had no trace of the dark brush, but he passed his engineering genes to a Negro. *(To EDGAR)* Haven't you heard of the quadroon balls, where to enter, a lady's skin has to be lighter than tan paper kept at the door.

EDGAR. *(Starting for the door)* That's appalling.

UNCLE MICHEL. Don't walk away while I am talking. You should avoid these *gens de colour* or free people.

(A SERVANT enters to turn up the oil lamps and the carved candlesticks.)

EDGAR. Free?

TELL. *(Starting for the door)* Intermediate in rights. Skin color between slaves and whites.

UNCLE MICHEL. Everyone is free now so free colored men are the same as other colored; no, they are worse, they are angry and they are a lot smarter. Am I right, America? Tell?

(SERVANT storms out.)

EDGAR. I'm very interested in Norbert's inventions. *(Abruptly turns to leave.)*

UNCLE MICHEL. Keep your distance, Edgar. We don't want a family hanging.

EDGAR. The citizens I fought with in the Commune died for—

UNCLE MICHEL. I'm fond of Norbert. We played together as boys. He's the one liable to get lynched.

(EDGAR goes out with TELL. UNCLE MICHEL hands a bill to RENÉ.)

UNCLE MICHEL. Invoices with no checks. Both used to come in one envelope. *(He exits)*

25

(Once he is gone, **AMERICA** *hurries over to* **RENÉ** *. He breaks away, and checks the doors and windows for eavesdroppers.)*

RENÉ. I can't talk now.

AMERICA. Tonight, usual place?

RENÉ. We must postpone our plans.

AMERICA. I don't want to wait any longer.

RENÉ. I can't leave Tell with the children alone.

AMERICA. I care about her children, about the whole household more than—

RENÉ. Tell is...pregnant.

AMERICA. She is...You got her pregnant? You...slept with her while I'm waiting?

RENÉ. She said she couldn't get...

AMERICA. You have...I thought you weren't intimate.

(Moves to her restlessly, motioning for her to keep her voice down)

RENÉ. Ah, sugar. I'm just as upset...

AMERICA. Ah, sugar. Don't touch me.

RENÉ. Now Edgar's here we'll repay you. I can't let our cotton business go under. *(Squeezing her hand)* Can't we talk later?

AMERICA. My husband's going to kill me if I don't give him that money right away. When he discovered it was missing he tore up the house looking for it. At night he rolls over and makes awful grunting sounds, cursing under his breath. Money and retaliation, that's all the judge cares about. One nod from him and I'm in prison or a mental hospital. If he finds out I stole that money...

(A burst of laughter comes from the pantry.)

DIDI. *(Offstage)* Where are you taking me?

(**EDGAR** *comes in carrying a birthday cake.* **DIDI** *follows coaxed by* **MATHILDE, TELL, UNCLE MICHEL** *and* **JO**)

ALL. SURPRISE!!

DIDI. I don't like surprises. I said I'm not celebrating.

JO. It's just three candles.

MATHILDE. *(Lighting the candles)* You are still on the sunny side of thirty.

UNCLE MICHEL. From now on you should freeze. Your mother was forty for years.

(**DIDI**, *half-reassured, blows out the candles*)

JO. Round the table you must go. You must go. Must go...it's your birthday.

UNCLE MICHEL. *(Glancing at* **EDGAR**) Let's give Didi a kiss.

(**EDGAR** *is about to do so when babies' crying comes from the rear hallway.* **RENÉ** *walks between* **DIDI** *and* **EDGAR** *spoiling the kiss.*)

RENÉ. Estelle. You think it's right to ignore the children? (**TELL** *turns her head, stung, jumps up, and starts out. He reaches for her arm, guiltily but she stiffens and keeps going past)* Take the cane. You're going to kill yourself, swear to God. I can't raise these monsters alone.

(**DIDI** *gives* **EDGAR** *a frustrated look and then leaves with* **MATHILDE** *and* **UNCLE MICHEL**)

RENÉ. *(to* **EDGAR**) My God, what's happening to me? I used to love children but I can't stand the sight of them. America, help Tell with the...

(**AMERICA** *exits.*)

EDGAR. You were the one with the vision of family life.

RENÉ. I've no vision. My creditors have it but I don't. *(Puts an arm around* **EDGAR** *and hugs him appreciatively.)* You've no idea of the hardship conditions here. You can't just go out and find clients. There is always someone who can get there before you. *(Takes a swig from his flask)* Country traders bartering cotton.

God knows who they are. Negotiating is getting ugly. Hell, I'd like nothing more than to get away from here as soon as possible.
(Another drink) When are you coming to the office?

EDGAR. I'm here to paint.

RENÉ. Couldn't you do that later...Hey...

EDGAR. I just gave you money...look...Cousin Norbert is here.

RENÉ. I can't work with him.

EDGAR. Why not? He could hire you to work on his... His sugar refining inventions are renowned.

RENÉ. It's not that simple. He can't do anything without facing threats.

EDGAR. From whom?

RENÉ. The White League. *(Glances uneasily to the entranceways with a change of tone)* They fight against the rising tide of colored people. Names like the Ku Klux Klan, the White Brotherhood, Camellias of Louisiana, mean anything to you? Uncle runs one white group. Our brother-in-law runs another.

EDGAR. *(His face hardens)* And you?

RENÉ. I'm involved also...I have to be.

EDGAR. This is what your Confederacy has given you?

RENÉ. You don't understand how it works here.

EDGAR. I fought for a dream. I joined the Commune because I believed all citizens were brothers.

RENÉ. Nice theory.

EDGAR. I still believe it. The White League is the opposite of everything the Commune fought and died for...

RENÉ. This is another world.

EDGAR. Then it's not mine.

(EDGAR exits.)

(AMERICA slumps against the pantry doorway.)

AMERICA. René, when are you going to tell your wife?

RENÉ. Right now, I can't. Tell is very fragile.

AMERICA. And me? What will happen to me?

(RENÉ grins at her provocatively, and takes a ring from his pocket)

AMERICA. A silver ring? I want you, I want a future, not a silver ring.

RENÉ. This isn't silver. It's platinum. Handmade in France. The jeweler was so snobbish I could barely talk to him.

(JO eavesdrops at the gallery window)

Later. Believe me, we'll talk later.

(AMERICA goes to the window, looking at the ring in dismay. She hears JO, looks up annoyed.)

AMERICA. What do you want anything?

JO. No.

(blackout)

(Slide then lights for street scene with another slide and music)

Scene Two

*(A week later at five o'clock, **EDGAR** and **TELL** stroll along the levee, twenty feet high and full of shadows.)*

TELL. You see Norbert?

EDGAR. No. The levee is full of whites. A giant lady with a parrot just sashayed by.

TELL. *(Laughing into her hand)* Any sign of a well-built brown man?

EDGAR. A tall white man just went by. He was very dashing in his checked jacket—

TELL. You like clothes?

(He laughs and squeezes her arm.)

EDGAR. When I paint. Colors set the tone.

TELL. Who's that up there scaling the levee?

EDGAR. Some white couples–the women in bustles and carrying parasols.

TELL. I like how you see things.

EDGAR. Precision is everything.

TELL. What time is it?

EDGAR. Don't worry. We're doing the right thing. Patience.

*(**EMILY**, a pretty middle-aged woman of color, sneaks in panting, nervous. She spots **EDGAR** by a street lamp, touches his shoulder, and draws him into the shadows.)*

EMILY. You don't recognize me?

TELL. No. Should I know you? You can't be Cousin Emily... Norbert's wife?

*(**EMILY** tosses back a hood, lifting off an alpaca turban.)*

EMILY. I'm Emily.

(EDGAR gives her an arresting smile and tips his cap.)

EDGAR. I'm Edgar. This is Tell.

TELL. We know each other. Should we go somewhere inside. We're so exposed here.

EMILY. Where?

EDGAR. *(EDGAR looks around.)* Here's fine. Where's your husband?

EMILY. *(Embarrassed)* Home. I took the back route. My legs got so cold, walking through the damp.

EDGAR. *(Noticeably upset)* He's not coming? Can you go back and get him?

EMILY. He's sick. Bad virus.

EDGAR. Well, I'll go to your home. I've got to see him.

TELL. Papa shouldn't have been so rude when Norbert came by—

EDGAR. I'll take Tell home and come back here if he'll meet me.

EMILY. *(Noticeably winded)* Norbert's a proud man . . .

EDGAR. Sit. Rest.

TELL. *(Startled)* No. Those benches used to be just for whites.

(EDGAR begins touching EMILY, wiping off rain from her shoulder.)

TELL. Keep your manner business-like.

(EMILY backs off and shakes out her drenched hem and petticoats.)

EMILY. You better get used to the rain. Don't look like New Orleans is ever going to dry out.

TELL. Take my hankie. You shouldn't have risked danger by coming here. A colored woman alone...

EMILY. Let's wait for these whites to pass... Norbert wants to move to Paris.

TELL. Keep walking.

EDGAR. Who'd have thought you'd have to meet this way after the war.

EMILY. Any Negro is a target. Doesn't matter if you are free.

(Offstage sound of soldiers passing with a hard stride.)

TELL. Union soldiers

EMILY. Hope they don't want to fight.

(Offstage. Sounds of a skirmish.)

TELL. We should go.

EDGAR. No. Not just yet.

EMILY. Better make Edgar understand.

TELL. Lets go closer to the river.

*(TELL leads **EDGAR** and **EMILY** away.)*

EMILY. Do Negroes keep apart in Paris?

EDGAR. No.

EMILY. Nobody lynches them? My dream is to go somewhere they don't punish you for your skin. Norbert deals with it better. It's been seven years since the War and the hatred's gotten worse. God knocked Saint Paul from his horse, but how many men fall and begin to see... in the South? Norbert says, "A new age is coming with shining, kind people. Inventions will multiply. Carriages and streetcars gonna' go by themselves." That's why we want to move to Paris, because people are more forward-thinking there.

*(Sound of horsemen riding along the river edge, brushing past them. **EMILY** wipes sweat from her lip, sticks the hankie back up her sleeve.)*

EMILY. If you'll excuse me, Miss Tell. I think you and your children should go back to Paris with Edgar. Leave this town and your...difficult situation. It ain't going to get any better.

TELL. *(Awkward)* I don' know—but I do miss Paris.

EMILY. I better go check on Norbert. *(She pulls down her turban over her shiny clamped hair.)* I tell myself I'm closing the book on one life to open it on another. I'll look at the river one last time. I fear I want something a woman can't have: equality.

TELL. Smart women shouldn't be in the South. It's difficult for whites and impossible for Negroes.

(EMILY turns to TELL, tears sprouting by her eyes.)

EMILY. I'd feel better if we travel with you and Edgar.

TELL. Oh, no. Not now. Not yet.

EDGAR. There are people I can't leave.

EMILY. I know it's hard. Inside, I want to scream. I have a sister and a mother, all from here. When that ship pulls off, that horn blows, and my mother waves, tears will burst me apart. I tell myself, serve as an example of a woman who got away. What do you think God wants me to do?

(SOUND: Chimes from Saint Louis Cathedral soar.)

EMILY. *(Withdrawing)* Terrible thunder. Looks like Satan's afoot.

TELL. You sure you want to go to Paris?

EMILY. Y'all come too. *(Lowering her voice)* We're dealing with evil that Yanks and the Freedmen's Bureau can't stop.

(They see men walk nearby in deer stalking caps and heavy lace-up boots. EMILY pulls up her hood.)

EMILY. Oh, Lord. We're being watched. By that fellow over there, and there. I better go.

EDGAR. They can't harm you. I'll make Uncle receive you—

EMILY. Don't go getting yourself shot. You dealing with some mean men. No one can stop—*(With bitter irony)* You haven't seen your Uncle's getup? He and Will are planning a battle. They are so mad they can't carry a gun and vote. *(Her voice trembling with rage)* They'll kill any Negro that tries to stand up, and any white man that helps him.

EDGAR. Yes, I know. My brother also. *(He reaches out shamefaced and takes her hand, but she drops it immediately)*

EMILY. Colored politicians can't save no one. You watch out.

TELL. *(Takes* **EMILY** *'s arm.)* I'll go home with you.

(Rain creeps down. **EDGAR** *swoopes up his umbrella.)*

EDGAR. I'll escort you both.

(Distant cries and a random gunshot hurl them back to reality.)

EMILY. No, it's best I go alone!

(She lifts her skirts, vanishes through the shadows and breaks free.)

(slide fades out)

(blackout)

Scene Three

(Two weeks later on the gallery. **UNCLE MICHEL** *sits boredly; behind him,* **JO** *crouches with her puppets, singing, putting warring puppets on his shoulders.* **MATHILDE** *and* **DIDI** *sit restlessly, sewing.)*

(Apart, **TELL** *relaxes into the pose* **EDGAR** *has created for her while he paints.)*

EDGAR. *(To* **TELL** *intimately)* I try to capture something deeply felt. I'm not the artist you knew. My energy doesn't always flow. And in Paris, the bad news is if you've been the new talent, they may think it's someone else's turn. I'm thirty-eight and haven't found the right—. Papa wants me to go to law school—...I thought I'd relocate here. Do landscapes. but I have a problem with your heat and sun. So I'm exploring faces and interiors. *(Brittle, pauses)* Only when painting you do I feel relaxed. Then it feels effortless to blend colors, lead white, Naples yellow, vermillion. To catch the shifting sun in less than an hour of painting time. To lay in the important masses...like the rocker on the gallery. I keep my eye on you and the world on canvas drifts magically into place.

UNCLE MICHEL. *(Calls out)* Shouldn't the painting session end?

DIDI. Isn't drawing in front of others disrespectful?

EDGAR. I don't think so. Since I joined the military, I always feel I'm painting apart.

UNCLE MICHEL. Edgar should paint you Didi.

*(***DIDI** *scoops up her embroidery and she and* **MATHILDE** *make a great business of sewing.)*

JO. *"Frere Jacques, frere Jacques, dormez-vous? Dormez-vous? Sonnez le matines. Sonnez le matines..."*

MATHILDE. If I were single, I'd marry Edgar. I would surely. Yes indeed.

DIDI. *(Embroidering diligently)* You've three children and a husband.

MATHILDE. I'm tired of living for them. Last night, I dreamed I was by Will's casket and I whispered, "Thanks for freeing me." And off I went to Paris. Does that mean my husband will get shot and die? It's awful."

UNCLE MICHEL. *(Affectionately reprimanding)* Come watch our puppet show. Someone needs to give Jo attention. Call all the children out.

MATHILDE. No. Not now.

UNCLE MICHEL. You don't want to see your children?

MATHILDE. I need some time with Edgar. Desiree will later.

DIDI. *(Stung)* No, I won't.

(With a baffled shrug of his shoulders, **UNCLE MICHEL** *leaves with* **JO.** **DIDI** *puts her sewing down.)*

DIDI. I'm waiting to read my writings to Edgar. Literature has always deeply interested him. Many of his paintings are based on Biblical, Classical and Romantic literature.

MATHILDE. So he'll be proposing soon?

DIDI. Our discussions are purely intellectual.

MATHILDE. How disappointing.

DIDI. *(Quickly)* Who knows? He admires women writers and protagonists. He reads repeatedly *Madame Bovary—*

(Focus swings to the gallery, **EDGAR** *painting* **TELL** *with an awkward uneasy tenderness)*

(SOUND: Something like Satie's music)

EDGAR. It's amazing. You have these moments of terrific intensity and utter passiveness. I can't wrap my mind around it. *(Coming over to her, he kneels and puffs her overskirts.)*

TELL. I wish I could see your drawing.

EDGAR. You mightn't like it. No, you...would. You're a good liar. I always felt I had to paint. But when you left Paris, painting seemed a necessity.

TELL. It's your gift!

EDGAR. I'm no prodigy. My talent comes through merciless work...

TELL. I used to watch you painting at the Louvre for hours.

EDGAR. I sensed you watching me.

TELL. You didn't.

EDGAR. That's where the extra red came in my "Daughters of Japheth." I was blushing.

TELL. It was a crush.

EDGAR. I was observing you even when you didn't know it.

TELL. I felt you, observing me.

EDGAR. I felt you...feeling me observing you. *(Laughs)* That's what painters do.

(The family exits the gallery. **EDGAR** *continues painting* **TELL***)*

EDGAR. *(Hesitates—then slowly)* Still there was something inexplicable—sacred in the way we connected.

TELL. You were lonely.

EDGAR. Don't diminish what I'm saying.

TELL. I wish I could see your painting.

EDGAR. *(He stares at her sheepishly, his voice drifting deep into himself)* When you touched my face earlier, I said nothing. But there's those intricacies of feeling even I can't understand. *(He continues painting)*

37

Scene Four

(Later, at the House. **RENÉ** *sits at the desk, struggling with bills.* **JO***, lying on the sofa, makes one of her puppets beat another.)*

PUPPET—JO. I've had enough of her. I'm going to do something to her. I'm not going to kill her but she's got to suffer.

AMERICA. *(From the pantry, calls out)* Jo!

*(***JO*** hides behind the sofa. Strolling in, speaks with peevishness)*

AMERICA. Come practice piano. She is always hiding somewhere. *(Pause)* Oh René. I went looking for you upstairs.

RENÉ. This place is turning into a nursery. I had to come down. I'm going to pay for my children to grow up, then I'm going to Paris and stay drunk.

AMERICA. *(Inches behind him, romantically)* How long can I be expected to take all this? Have you talked to Edgar?

RENÉ. I can't yet. Look...You're married too.

AMERICA. What kind of marriage do I have? At least before the war my husband never worried about money, because there was always more, more. Now he counts every penny. My grandma used to say what would you rather be, an old man's darling or a young man's bride? I settled for the old man's darling, but now I'm not even that. He thinks because I worked in the kitchen before, I should be grateful. *(Sits on* **RENÉ***'s lap, throws her arms around his neck.)* I'm young. I want to travel. He never expected me to want that. I'm so bored. When he talks, it's only to repeat himself or say something ugly. He hates everybody I like and one day all his meanness will come out at me. When it does, I'm a dead woman. We've got to leave. When will you talk to Edgar?

RENÉ. How can I leave when the pregnancy is in trouble? *(There is a silence in which* **RENÉ** *moves away awkwardly. A strange aloofness comes over him.)* What time do the guests arrive at your house?

AMERICA. They're not coming.

RENÉ. But I'm supposed to introduce Edgar to...new clients.

AMERICA. I canceled the Christmas party.

RENÉ. You decided not to have it.

AMERICA. You won't leave your wife and give me back my money.

RENÉ. What?

AMERICA. I had to accuse my servants of theft. The judge sent them to jail.

RENÉ. But... You were supposed to—help me get money from the judge—

AMERICA. His friends have no money. They're looking for money from you.

RENÉ. Everybody cannot be broke. Some people have inherited money.

AMERICA. Yes, but the rich really love their money. They'll turn from you.

RENÉ. So you're calling off the Christmas party?

AMERICA. To which I'm barely invited, although it's at my house. I'm the servant who happens to own the house. I don't act like one of y'all. But Tell's the angel mother. If I've to hear once more about her first husband being nephew to Jefferson Davis—

RENÉ. You said the judge would lend money, if Edgar approached him.

AMERICA. Yes, but we haven't had relations in eight months.

RENÉ. You think it's fair to punish me? You know I'd love to run off with you. Never look at this wanting house again. How can I act dishonorably? So many people are depending on me. Every night when I go to bed I imagine you alongside me. Every other second I think of you. When I'm shaving, combing my hair, stepping off the gallery, hopping on the streetcar, opening the office door, picking up the mail. *(He gives a little despairing laugh)* There's hardly an action I do without daydreaming about you. That's my personal torture.

AMERICA. Well you'll just have to bear it.

*(*RENÉ* gives her a dark look and exits.* JO *sneaks out onto the gallery, frowning, leaving a puppet behind.* AMERICA *watches her, then picks up the puppet and throws it and walks out)*

(Outside it thunders, and rains. Moments later, **MATHILDE** *and* **JO** *come in with a vase of red gladioli.)*

JO. It's true, I did see Mr. René and America kissing here. They're gone but they were here, kissing.

MATHILDE. My. They are just good friends.

JO. Good friends don't kiss so long...Is she going to have a baby?

MATHILDE. Heavens no. It's Christmas time. People are drinking, full of friendliness.

*(***JO*** tries to look in her aunt's eyes, but she keeps them averted, arranging the flowers)*

MATHILDE. Some things you can't understand until you grow up. Now let's get you dressed for the Christmas party.

*(***MATHILDE*** coaxes* **JO** *out to the front hallway as* **TELL** *comes in the rear parlor dressed in splendid velvet and satin, her pregnancy heightening her voluptuous sensuality. On hearing the rain and thunder, she adjusts her sleeves with a forlorn gentleness.)*

*(**SOUND:** Christmas music plays, something like "Oh Holy Night," as* **TELL** *moves to the desk and smells the vase of red gladioli)*

*(**LIGHTS:** Lights dim and a slide is displayed briefly)*

*(***EDGAR*** comes in from the back parlor. A pause. His expression becomes thoughtful, almost as if he's seeing the painting, "Portrait of Estelle")*

TELL. Edgar. I know it is you.

EDGAR. How is that?

TELL. By your footsteps.

EDGAR. Is that it?

TELL. Well, actually there's an energy.

EDGAR. Can you sense what I'm doing?

TELL. It feels like you're watching me. It's rude to stare.

EDGAR. I'm taking in the whole picture.

TELL. May I get you something?

EDGAR. Just your company.

TELL. Perhaps we should have champagne.

EDGAR. You're all dressed in a rose-colored gown.

TELL. I mostly wear black.

EDGAR. Come here. Let me see.

TELL. *(Crosses to* **EDGAR***)* I've clothes I've never worn simply because I don't know what they look like anymore. For tonight I tried on every gown in my armoire.

EDGAR. I love fine fabrics, the softness on the skin. Let's sit here.

*(***TELL** *moves away and bumps into the sofa. He pauses, struggling with himself. Outside it thunders and rain drops down.)*

EDGAR. Could you tell me how the blindness first began? I won't tell anyone.

TELL. I began knocking glasses of water off the table. I couldn't tell where the ends of things were—tables, steps.

EDGAR. What did you do...at first?

TELL. I denied it...Nothing is so good or so bad as you think it is going to be.

EDGAR. *(His face tenses)* I've never spoken about this to anyone, afraid to acknowledge it and make it stronger. I've been plagued with headaches. At first, I thought it was an empathetic response. I was suffering with you. Then I blamed the weather. It's unusually hot. Temperatures in December, I thought you had in June. I've had a sudden drop in vision. The less light in the room, the less I can distinguish. Colors and details blur. My right eye is mostly worthless. They say you don't know what you have unless you lose it. Well, painters know our eyes are important. There is always that fear, so when it happens it's traumatic.

41

TELL. Maybe you should see a doctor.

EDGAR. Doctors know everything and nothing. What if I can't paint anymore? What if—if I lose the other eye? My God, no. You just woke up one morning, blind? I couldn't face it.

TELL. After two operations, they put a sharp object into my eye...But your headaches are probably from New Orleans and the heat. Paint indoors.

(He remains hopelessly silent. She adds sadly)

You've two options: not paint or work with your limitations here.

EDGAR. What choice is that?

TELL. A hard one, but I think you see from inside. Painting comes from *(Points to her heart)* here. *(She smiles strangely)* You'll use all your senses, your hearing, your touch. I see you more clearly, now, than ever before.

EDGAR. That's what I miss the most—your optimistic attitude.

(Outside the rain intensifies.)

*(***AMERICA*** comes in from the pantry.)*

AMERICA. I'm sorry. Edgar, we must talk—

(From the hallway, we hear **MATHILDE, DIDI** *and* **JO** *singing something like, "Oh Holy Night" as they enter.)*

AMERICA. I've canceled the party. What with the rain, the heat...Every few seconds this nasty thunder.

DIDI. But I counted on this evening. For one night I wouldn't have to be the household nun.

AMERICA. I told the servants to send the guests away.

DIDI. Well there goes my plan to recite Baudelaire.

MATHILDE. Why don't you recite for the family.

DIDI. Well, why not? *(Crosses to the center of the room. Reciting:)* "Woman... for the artist...is the object of keenest admiration and curiosity that the picture of life can offer its contemplator. No doubt woman is sometimes a light, a glance, an invitation to happiness, sometimes just a word; but above all she is a general harmony, not only in her bearing and the way in which she moves and walks, but also in the muslin, the gauzes...

*(A pounding at the door. **JO** runs for it. Two **MEN** step in, with a metallic sound to their walk. They are costumed in white silk duke's costumes, high leather boots, plumed hats, curtain masks, gloves. Two other masked **MEN**, possibly actors playing **UNCLE MICHEL** and **EMILY** wait by the door.)*

MAN #1. We're with the White League.

MAN #2. Is Michel Musson home?

DIDI. My father? No.

MAN #1. Anyone seen Mr. Norbert Rillieux? They say he's cousin to you people.

*(**EDGAR** goes back to drawing. The **MEN** march before the painting.)*

MAN #2. Emily Rillieux. She here? Somebody says she has left town.

*(**JO** runs to **EDGAR**.)*

MAN #1. *(To **EDGAR**)* Who are you?

TELL. This is our cousin Edgar Degas. His Mama was an American.

MAN #2. *(To **EDGAR**)* Against the law to harbor foreigners. How long you been here?

*(**EDGAR** passes them his official papers.)*

MAN #2. These passes are good for three months.

TELL. He's getting those renewed next week. There's that extension, remember.

*(The **MEN** eye each other and grumble.)*

MAN #1. If it wasn't for your father, we'd have him deported.

(TELL's **SISTERS** *and* **JO** *rush over.)*

MAN #2. You got too many relatives in this house. We've got a warrant and we'll check for more.

(The **MEN** *burrow offstage and come back on, dumping drawers, scattering papers, and clothes.* **EDGAR** *swoops up fallen objects, cursing in French.)*

TELL. *(To* **EDGAR***)* Hold back. It'll be worse for us, if you don't.

EDGAR. *(To* **MEN***)* Watch what you do!

*(***MAN #1** *comes to* **EDGAR** *as if to strike)*

MAN #1. Some say you been meeting Negroes on the levee. They said you been conducting business. That's not allowed.

EDGAR. I thought Negroes were free.

(They fight. **TELL** *darts to him.)*

TELL. My cousin is new here. He doesn't mean harm. He doesn't understand.

MAN #2. You teach him. There are laws here—

*(***TELL** *gets the* **MEN** *some lemonade and biscuits. They step aside, drink to the bottom.)*

MAN #1. Those Negroes bother you, you let us know.

(The **MEN** *patrol about. The marching offstage goes on.)*

TELL. Pretend all is normal.

*(***RENÉ** *enters as if inebriated. He ushers the* **MEN** *out. We see one of them is* **WILL.** **RENÉ** *stands in the doorway.)*

RENÉ. *(To* **TELL***)* I told y'all to stay clear of the Negroes. Whatever you did I don't want to know. But it's got to stop...You want to get us all killed?

*(***TELL** *fans herself and moves to the sofa.* **EDGAR** *exits.* **AMERICA** *fidgets, looks remotely in* **RENÉ***'s direction)*

44

RENÉ. I'll walk you home. A terrible storm's coming. I didn't expect it. It hasn't rained in weeks. *(Pats* **TELL***'s cheek in dismissal, huskily, forcing a smile)* Don't wait up. *(Follows* **AMERICA** *out)*

JO. *(Trails them with her puppets)* Kiss me, kiss me.

MATHILDE. Put those up. Come with me.

TELL. Let her stay.

*(***MATHILDE** *turns away with a tense laugh and goes out.* **TELL** *walks somberly to the sofa.* **JO** *tiptoes behind her.)*

JO. Can I comb your hair, Mama?

TELL. Yes, there is a brush on the desk.

JO. Mama.

TELL. Yes?

JO. Never mind. *(With a probing look)* What was Papa like?

TELL. I've told you this before, Jo. Your father was good-looking, dashing. I picked him from a circle of carefree southern boys, now mostly dead.

JO. Do you miss Papa now you've a second husband?

TELL. That was a long time ago.

JO. What's it like being married? Do you kiss a lot?

TELL. Sometimes.

JO. Do married people kiss other people too?

TELL. Yes, but differently. So many questions.

JO. Who do you love most? Papa or Mr. René?

TELL. I love you most, that's all you have to worry about.

45

JO. I want a real Papa, not a pretend Papa. *(She reaches out and grasps* **TELL***'s arm)*

TELL. And the babies? Don't they need their real Papa?

JO. I never thought about them. *(She gives a little sad sigh)* Does it hurt having babies?

TELL. Sometimes. You arrived fighting, your face red. Your uncle, Jefferson Davis, sent me a diamond pin, a swan with green eyes—

JO. Why did you marry Mr. René and not Uncle Edgar?

TELL. René played the part of the successful young banker. So handsome and so smart. He'd been to his tailor and bought the costume. Suntan suits in summer, a scarf thrown over his shoulder to give the impression he was rushing. He flitted around the edge of single ladies, not knowing he'd get caught in the web of a blind woman.

JO. *(Stares at her, puzzled)* You like being married?

TELL. The best part is anticipation. Hearing a man's footsteps at your door.

*(***MATHILDE*** comes in from the rear parlor door, frowns admonishingly)*

MATHILDE. This isn't talk for a child.

TELL. She's mine. Besides, she understands everything.

JO. I do. *(Bell jingles)* That's Uncle Will. With the little Christmas tree. He promised we could trim it with Uncle Edgar.

*(***JO*** runs off into the hallway)*

*(***DIDI*** walks in with **MATHILDE** and **JO***)*

DIDI. A message for Mathilde. I didn't open it.

*(***DIDI*** leaves taking **JO**. A loose smile twists **MATHILDE***'s face as she reads the note again.)*

MATHILDE. There'll be no tree.

TELL. Will won't be home tonight? Is he with...

MATHILDE. Don't mention her name. All men cheat. When Will went to the altar, instead of saying "I do," he should have said, "I'll try." Certain women become the strange attractors.

TELL. Why do men think they can get away with it?

MATHILDE. Because they can.

TELL. How do you handle it?

MATHILDE. There is a sense of relief when you know, but you never admit it. I light a candle, recall my licentious thoughts. It's good for wives to reflect in silence. If we can't save ourselves, perhaps we can save our children.

TELL. I couldn't cope...

MATHILDE. Men are hunters. They aren't capable of loving a woman, much less of telling her they do, or of doing anything about it.

TELL. That's not true. There are men who can love.

MATHILDE. Edgar, again?

TELL. I didn't say that...Aren't you tired of standing at the door, wringing your hands, asking your husband to talk to you till your voice sounds like thunder?

MATHILDE. I've suffered loneliness for sure but I've lots of tasks done for me so I can keep my shine. Wives have to look good, so as our husbands age, we can replace their mistresses and become their mothers, perfecting the technique of living with them while they're ignoring us. The home should be a wife's sanctuary. I try to shift the routine by putting breezy surprises into every day, a Christmas ornament. An Easter bouquet. Nothing unpleasant. I dare not mention the loan to René.

TELL. He's repaid you, hasn't he?

MATHILDE. No, and now I find out...he hasn't paid the bills for three months, nor has he spoken to Edgar about a loan.

TELL. For God's sake...take this. *(TELL yanks off her ring)*

MATHILDE. *(Refusing the ring)* Not your diamond. Anyway, it's nothing. A drop in the river.

(MATHILDE goes out the pantry doors. Thunder intensifies. Moments later, EDGAR enters, carefully watches TELL for a moment, then walks slowly to where she sits. She looks tired, miserably sad.)

EDGAR. It's Edgar. Are you all right?

TELL. *(Rejecting him)* I'm fine. I'm in alone time. It's necessary, it's difficult, but it's here. *(Pause)* See me in the morning, and I'll have a little repartee with you.

EDGAR. *(Goes to the window, watches the rain as if talking aloud to himself)* Such a cold moon night. A brittle moon, stone blue. Like your wedding night. The hard darkness of the Cathedral almost gobbles up your bright gown as you come down the aisle. I get there an hour before the others just so...I can be ready...for what I don't know. Why'd you—marry René?

TELL. I had a small child...He was willing to live in America.

EDGAR. Off your Papa's money...

TELL. Didn't Didi write?

EDGAR. Yes, but she hardly mentioned you. *(He takes her hand with deep caring)* I wish I could have been there with you when you lost your sight.

TELL. Me too.

EDGAR. I would have been your eyes. You could have counted on me.

(TELL clutches her stomach in pain. Startled, EDGAR looks about nervously and helps her to the sofa. She looks up at him. Stricken with a cramp, she stiffens, patting his hand.)

EDGAR. Let me call someone.

TELL. No. Now that I've got you here alone, stay with me. Closer. Be with me. Bless me, Father, for I have sinned. For so long I've dreamed of having you here like this, your face by mine. Your hand here. *(A spasm of pain crosses her face. She squeezes his hand in hers)*

EDGAR. Let me call Mathilde.

TELL. Since you came, I can't sleep. I barely eat and I feel full. Yesterday, I sat before you while you painted, heard the brush on the canvas, smelled the oils, felt your voice all around me and I was totally happy. I wanted to sit there forever.

EDGAR. Please. Don't talk. Let me call your sister.

TELL. I don't want to move or wake up for fear you'll be gone. I want to live here in this dream.

EDGAR. *(He reacts to her pain, blurting out, finally unrestrained.)* When René told me he'd marry you, I accepted it. I adored him, so why shouldn't he have you...Up to the last minute, I thought, prayed you might cancel. The most difficult thing was to say congratulations. Because till I said that you weren't really married. Hearing you say, "I do," I...I...My body felt like stone.

TELL. People said you were ill.

EDGAR. I blamed it on a fever, yes. I told myself I'd get through it if I didn't see you. To stay away at all costs. Don't write. Don't—But when I went back to painting, my perspectives were off. I've said about all I can say without—

TELL. You never proposed. I waited...and waited.

EDGAR. You preferred him. Admit it.

TELL. René was carefree with a childish grandiosity. True. And you sat in the corner with your paintings, quiet, unpredictable, even defiant.

EDGAR. I couldn't look at you and speak at the same time. And after you left, I kept in motion, traveling about—Rome, London, Madrid—even their visual splendor couldn't keep my eyes from loving you. Let me call your sisters.

TELL. No...stay with me. One more moment. *(Another intense cramp)*
OH MY GOD. OH NO. OH MY GOD.

(blackout)

ACT TWO

Scene One

(Slide up of the Degas house, then romantic music like the composition of Erik Satie and lights at the same time, out)

*(***JO*** is on the floor dancing in her dreams, ***RENÉ*** sits wearily at his desk, rises, walks slowly out like an old man. Sounds of flooding rain. **JO** crawls onto the sofa like a scared little girl. **DIDI** and **MATHILDE** come in from the rear hallway, **DIDI** whispering roughly to hide her tense nerves.)*

DIDI. I can't sleep. These last six weeks with Tell have been so hard.

MATHILDE. Nor can I. America's hatred level spikes at night. How did she take over the house?

DIDI. She runs René. The woman who runs the man, runs the house. *(Looks through the parlor toward the window where the rain pours)* If only Edgar would take me to Paris.

MATHILDE. Bring me and the children too.

DIDI. How did everything go wrong? I was a joyful person.

MATHILDE. Perhaps Edgar can figure it out.

DIDI. You've been hit too many times...I can't talk to anyone anymore, and we used to chat into the night. Now if I say anything, it erupts into a fight.

MATHILDE. Edgar's the only nice one—

DIDI. You must protect yourself. We were schooled for a better life. Men took care of women. Men were generally mean, but they took care of us. Now, they don't care for us and they're mean.

MATHILDE. Who knows which way is better, with or without a husband.

DIDI. *(Lowering her voice)* Come in my room when he's violent. You suffer more than Mama did.

MATHILDE. Papa didn't beat her.

DIDI. No. But their marriage was based on her obedience. Show those bruises to Papa.

MATHILDE. Will would deny it or blame Edgar. He shames anyone who won't join the White League. *(She turns her head away)* I keep wishing for Will to get shot. In a duel; collapse with a heart attack. Bless me, Father, for I have sinned.

(AMERICA comes in with an irritated glance around the front parlor. With a hard obstinate set to her face, she walks over to JO, and yanks her sheets off. JO scrunches into the sofa.)

AMERICA. Jo, get up.

JO. I'm sleepy.

AMERICA. We've got homeless all over the house. Your grandpa keeps letting them in because of the flood. There's a break in the levee. Can't you be useful—?

DIDI. She's just a child. She's—

AMERICA. *(Ignoring, DIDI—resentfully)* A bully. Bully, bully!

DIDI. I'll take over. *(Quickly)* Shush. Tell needs her rest, she's still hemorrhaging.

AMERICA. *(Turning to DIDI)* And you and Edgar encourage this —Jo's lazy! Totally spoiled, mentally unstable.

JO. I'm not!

AMERICA. She should be off on her uncle's grand estate—

DIDI. Filled with war veterans, amputees, victims of malaria.

AMERICA. Jo can't live in the nursery. Yesterday she threw a pair of—

JO. Little Will punched me and Gaston threw...my puppets out the window...

AMERICA. I've a headache, which Jo has given me. I've had one for two days.

JO. Uncle Edgar says you should go home!

AMERICA. And leave this house unattended? *(Screams)* Jo should leave before things get worse.

(UNCLE MICHEL approaches, tipsy—swaying in the front parlor doorway—in a loud voice)

UNCLE MICHEL. What's going on here? Will's drunk and the children are running around. *(To **DIDI**)* You should be with Edgar.

DIDI. Go to bed, Papa.

AMERICA. Mathilde's husband gambles and drinks. Edgar couldn't straighten him out.

*(They watch **UNCLE MICHEL**'s wavering progress through the front parlor. He goes out)*

AMERICA. That old man's a drunk too.

DIDI. Please show my father some respect.

*(**DIDI** and **JO** go out the front parlor door after **UNCLE MICHEL**, and **AMERICA** stomps off through the rear parlor door. **RENÉ**, clutching a baby, enters from the gallery, turns, watching the rain. Sips from his flask. Moments later **MATHILDE** slips in from the pantry with a bassinet.)*

MATHILDE. Did you get the doctor?

RENÉ. In whose boat? There's six feet of water out there.

MATHILDE. You've been drinking.

RENÉ. I've got to have a few drinks to start the day. How's Tell?

MATHILDE. Her bleeding's slowed.

RENÉ. Doctor doesn't want Tell to get too attached, because...

MATHILDE. I know.

RENÉ. Poor little thing is struggling to breathe. Oh my God. I'd like to help it—comfort Tell, but—I never wanted this baby, and she knew it. Her name's Jeanne, but she's no fighter. She hardly opens her eyes. When I put my finger in her fist, she barely squeezes. I rub her stomach, but she hardly notices. *(Terrified)* If only I'd acted enthusiastic, gotten more loans, things might have turned out all—

MATHILDE. Maybe not.

RENÉ. They say with Jeanne's pneumonia, it'll be a sweet painless end. It'll get harder for her to breathe until she stops. I hope I don't have to see it.

MATHILDE. Does Tell know?

RENÉ. I had to fake some slight hope for her.

MATHILDE. You gave her hope?

RENÉ. What else could I do? The woman keeps waiting for good news. Yesterday I was a banker's son in Paris. Women sparkled about me, sent me perfumed notes, anonymous flowers. I thought I'd come to Louisiana and Tell's father would make me a southern planter. Louisiana was the New World. Where you could be a success by age thirty. Yesterday I was a superficial dreamer. That was the real me. *(Uneasy now—with alcoholic talkativeness)* What did I find when I got here? Lazy people too lost to help me. Mosquitoes, moths and caterpillars dropping from trees. A bitter humidity, thousand-leg spiders, termites gobbling all they see. Prehistoric roaches. A stifling heat. A river waiting to burst its banks full of alligators and moccasins, and water rats fleeing up the oak trees. Children dropping with yellow fever, scarlet fever, typhoid. Unnamed infections. Hurricanes, floods, and infants struggling to breathe. *(MATHILDE puts her arm around him)* I suppose I must order a little casket.

MATHILDE. Yes, you must.

RENÉ. *(Taking a swig from his flask)* Thank God for alcohol. Things seem pinker, calmer. Soon in a room of death you are peacefully alone.

MATHILDE. Is that what you want?

RENÉ. Yes.

MATHILDE. No, you don't. You want to be with someone else.

*(RENÉ holds up a hand, then walks out heavily with the bassinet. She stares after him with worry and irritation. Seconds later, **UNCLE MICHEL** blusters into the room, his eyes glassy)*

53

UNCLE MICHEL. I can't sleep.

MATHILDE. My God, Papa, go back to bed.

UNCLE MICHEL. Where's René going? We have a White League meeting today. He's supposed to bring Edgar.

MATHILDE. Leave René alone.

UNCLE MICHEL. He's probably going back to sleep. He works from a part of his brain which is least developed.Oh well, maybe he's a good fighter, that's his last hope.

MATHILDE. Leave him alone!

(DIDI hurries in through the front parlor doors.)

DIDI. Where's René? Did he take the baby?

(MATHILDE leaves discreetly through the pantry as EDGAR enters quietly through the rear parlor doors. DIDI spots him, lowering her voice to a delighted tone of whispered confidence.)

DIDI. There you are. Papa is drinking. Will has smoked up all the cigars... I'll have to declare myself sick to get rest. And it's still raining.

EDGAR. Steadily. *(Tenderly)* I'll be leaving soon.

DIDI. How soon is soon?

EDGAR. Next week.

DIDI. Couldn't you stay a little longer?

EDGAR. It's time.

DIDI. Could I ask you something?

(UNCLE MICHEL rises, fighting a tipsy drowsiness.)

DIDI. It's about this novel that I am writing.

(Intrigued, UNCLE MICHEL grins and sits again)

DIDI. The story is about a woman who wants to be a writer, live in Paris. Is it possible, for a woman to have her own Bohemian garret?

EDGAR. Yes, but artists' studios are small, unheated, with a horrifying amount of dust and dirt.

DIDI. So she lives in this poor garret, and finds artists who are supportive—

EDGAR. Let's not forget jealous. In that crowd, everyone is in competition with everyone else.

DIDI. Despite others' envy, she enjoys literary soirées, does public lectures in Normandy—

EDGAR. Normandy?

DIDI. She meets a man, a painter who fought in the Commune.

UNCLE MICHEL. *(Rises annoyed)* What nonsense, Didi!

*(**UNCLE MICHEL** goes out. **DIDI** becomes pathetically relieved and eager)*

DIDI. She falls in love with this man...and they marry.

EDGAR. I was in love with all the Musson sisters.

DIDI. And we with you—

EDGAR. I couldn't get enough of you and Tell. Beautiful Tell, so young, already a mother and war widow. Such a stricken face, the tightness of her lips, the untidy strands of hair. Her eyes, deeply shadowed, downcast, always wet as if bleeding for that young captain sent to slaughter. I couldn't look at her without thinking that face filled the eyes of a dying man.

DIDI. You couldn't forget her face?

EDGAR. I had no concept of what loss could be till I saw this vision. No matter what I brought to captivate her, *bon-bons, marrons glacées,* she found no consolation. No comfort. Even now weak and suffering.

DIDI. She's the one...

EDGAR. You're right. She's the brave one. I'm the coward. *(Kneels by her, takes her hand)* I made a mistake. I never should have lost Tell to René.

(UNCLE MICHEL comes in through a gallery window. EDGAR is on his knee in front of DIDI. Triumphant, fighting the effect of his last drink, UNCLE MICHEL blushes and bursts out:)

UNCLE MICHEL. Didi, why don't you get downstairs. Baby's screaming. *(To EDGAR)* I would like to offer a toast but our liquor supply is shot.

EDGAR. We had wine in the cupboard.

UNCLE MICHEL. No more, it's drunk up.

(JO runs in from the gallery. She grabs her aunt's arm)

JO. Aunt Didi. Gaston's picking on me.

DIDI. *(With a loose, twisted smile)* All right. I'm coming.

(JO pulls her off onto the gallery. UNCLE MICHEL stares after them, looks suspiciously at EDGAR, goes out the front parlor door, baffled. Moments later, TELL rushes in from the pantry.)

TELL. Edgar, is that you?

EDGAR. Yes.

TELL. Oh my God. I can't find my baby. Why did they move her?

EDGAR. Mathilde just took her—

TELL. But she needs me to hold her. How can they take her from me without asking?

EDGAR. You were sleeping.

TELL. The baby needs me. If she misses me too much she may lose heart. Has her fever gone up?

(She moves about worriedly, speaking with a tone of concern, burying her face in her hands miserably. He stares at her sheepishly and shakes his head)

EDGAR. They wanted to spare you. Come here.

TELL. They've taken her off to die.

EDGAR. No one would do that.

TELL. Is her breathing worse? Did the doctor ever get here?

EDGAR. He's on his way.

TELL. Damn floods. No one can get in or out.

EDGAR. Come. Sit with me.

TELL. You're the only one who talks to me. René hasn't said a word since Jeanne was born. I don't think he likes her.

EDGAR. Jeanne's...in the sick room.

TELL. Isolation, that's the first step...She'll stop eating. Without me, she won't eat.

EDGAR. But you're weak.

TELL. I know. My milk is bad. I'm an unfit mother. I fed the others. Something is wrong. I cried without stopping since she was born. Now I can't even feed her. I called her Jeanne, after the Maid of Orleans, because I wanted her to be strong. But I've got to face it. She's not. What will I do if she passes?

EDGAR. She's a little better.

TELL. Don't lie. Not you too.

EDGAR. *(Takes her hands and gently seats her.)* Here, sit.

TELL. I want my girlhood back. The Paris Opera, the ballet, the racetrack. I want to see dancers turning in white tutus. Arabian stallions. You drew so well.

(Light changes)

EDGAR. If you move to Paris, I'd buy you a stallion and we'd ride it.

(Music and slides of Paris during his speech)

EDGAR. I'd take you to the opera, the ballet, the popular theater, and—

(Music and slides out when she sits up)

TELL. That's what I miss. Nonsense. Nonsense and seeing your work.

EDGAR. I'll take you to my studio, show you my modeling in wax. I'd put each piece in your hands. I'd teach you. I've been holding your words close. They've been driving me, whispering to me, filling my thoughts with hope. I've had to face a lot of emotions I've been painting about obliquely for a long time.

TELL. Don't give me hope for something that's never going to happen.

EDGAR. It's hard to confess but I have to...And you? I love you.

(EDGAR goes slowly out the front parlor. Moments later, **DIDI** *comes in from the back parlor.)*

DIDI. Tell...are you all right?

TELL. Yes, I'm fine. Didi, I must tell you something. I know it's wrong. There's no excusing it. But I always tell the truth, which endears me to no one.

DIDI. It's about Edgar.

TELL. Yes. First I...I admired his persistence...his commitment to painting contemporary life. What ferments in his head is breathtaking. I'm scared of it, and awed by it at the same time. Then I loved his...his humility. He's uncertain about the quality of his earlier works. Astonishing paintings of ballet rehearsals and horse races as I recall them. Then I appreciated his loneliness, assessing in middle age what he wants to do with his life. With him it's visceral—it goes beyond language—it's crazy, it's wonderful, that at my age, with my difficulties, Edgar loves me and I love him.

DIDI. You've already had two husbands, it's not fair.

TELL. I'd forgotten what it's like to feel valued.

DIDI. So you have to steal Edgar. You...you seduced him. You know how to fix yourself up—how to flirt—There are no men left since the war...You knew I wanted Edgar. How could you?

TELL. I couldn't help myself.

DIDI. That's no excuse. I can't wash away the unwanted birthdays. Men say they want intelligent women, but they don't, not really. Edgar and I are perfect for each other. The same artistic ambitions. I'd be happy just living with him, writing my stories. But with you flaunting yourself, he doesn't see me. *(In a burst of rage, she grabs her sister by the arm and twists it till* **TELL** *falls backwards)* Your own husband's having an affair with America, and you don't see. You lie there, doing nothing, feeling sorry for this baby you should never have had. Where do you think that sickly baby is? In my room. I'm the one who's got to watch it die. You're a saint while I'm just a woman without a husband. No matter I sit up nights writing. My eyes burn while you lie there in your lace and satin, flaunting those nightgowns René bought you. And you know that he did it out of guilt because he's seeing America. I've been dreaming of Edgar, prayed he'd come for me, but he never stopped loving you. There is a bridge between our past and our present. Somehow when he arrived, like lightning you and he were connected all over again.

(DIDI chokes huskily, sobs overcoming her, as she barrels out to the hallway. **MATHILDE***, who is coming in, shrinks back, then calls back to* **DIDI** *uneasily)*

MATHILDE. Didi, is something wrong? *(To* **TELL***)* Are you feeling worse again? *(Beat)* You can tell me.

TELL. Leave me alone.

(MATHILDE goes out into the hallway, yelling indignantly)

MATHILDE. Desiree, Desiree?!

TELL. Where's my baby? René! René! René!

(RENÉ dashes down the stairs)

RENÉ. *(To* **MATHILDE***)* May I have a moment with my wife?

MATHILDE. Yes of course. *(Exits)*

TELL. I've had a terrible shock. I learned something that I... I can't believe.

RENÉ. From whom? Mathilde?

TELL. No. Now tell me the truth. Don't lie to me.

RENÉ. I won't.

TELL. I just learned that you have been having relations with America.

RENÉ. Who told you that?

TELL. Is it true?

RENÉ. We're friends.

TELL. Did you make love to her?

RENÉ. How could you believe such... gossip.

TELL. Did you touch her?

RENÉ. America is... loyal.

TELL. Kiss her?

RENÉ. How can you think that? This is vicious gossip.

TELL. Liar! Liar! Liar!

(MATHILDE runs in the front parlor door. She sees RENÉ moving to the rear parlor door and comes round to TELL, touches her shoulder tenderly)

MATHILDE. Tell?

TELL. *(Loudly to MATHILDE and RENÉ)* I thought that America was a fine person. Sometimes I felt queasy when she was overly solicitous of René...Still, I told myself don't be small-minded because she is so good with the children. *(Pause)* Now I've got to accept the fact that while I was being nice, she was sleeping with my husband. Or so Didi says. René denies it?

(RENÉ signals to MATHILDE to lie for him. Without turning from RENÉ, MATHILDE says sharply)

MATHILDE. He's a coward.

(RENÉ shrugs, and slouches by the rear parlor door)

TELL. *(To* **MATHILDE***)* You knew? You knew and you didn't tell me? You were protecting René. Lord. I'm your sister. You and Didi have been covering for him.

MATHILDE. For God's sake. Everyone knew about it but you...and maybe Edgar.

TELL. Tell him too! Inform the world.

UNCLE MICHEL. *(Comes in from the pantry, letting the door slam)* What is happening in my house? In the old days women knew how to behave.

MATHILDE. Papa, go to bed.

*(***MATHILDE** *and* **TELL** *go out the front parlor doors. Once they have gone,* **UNCLE MICHEL** *marches to* **RENÉ***, hands him an envelope.* **RENÉ** *ducks away and goes to the desk.* **UNCLE MICHEL** *exits, slamming the door behind him.)*

(Seconds later, **EDGAR** *enters, crosses to the desk and takes the bill from* **RENÉ***.)*

EDGAR. It doesn't look like you've paid back any of Papa's loans.

RENÉ. I can't talk about anything else today

EDGAR. *(Examining another document)* Have you been selling cotton without exacting a commission?

RENÉ. I contacted our creditors. I did everything short of sending a drawing with a gun to my temple saying "Pay this or I'll kill myself." I didn't create the financial panic. I've had a short and sorry business life. I don't speak the language, I don't get the nuances of these cotton people. I just want to leave. If it wasn't for Tell, I'd have left Louisiana. *(With sudden foolish bravado)* I don't know a single person who wouldn't leave if the means were at hand. The French Quarter is the end of New Orleans, which is the end of Louisiana, which is the end of the world. We're standing at the end of the end.

EDGAR. I'm trying to get some clarity.

RENÉ. So you can report to Papa what you did right and I did wrong.

EDGAR. I'm the one who influenced Papa and our sisters and brother to invest in cotton, but you've the control over all the business. That's what Papa wanted—

RENÉ. I had to get Papa's power of attorney to keep us from starving.

EDGAR. Double-dealing will put you in jail.

RENÉ. Papa loaned me money. But he also financed the girls' marriages, your never-ending studies, and the Confederacy. Papa wanted to turn to you, but trusting me was all he had. Our grandfathers were the geniuses, not him. They made the fortunes in Louisiana cotton and Italian investments. He just inherited their nest egg.

EDGAR. Poor fellow trusted you. You came home raving about Louisiana and telling us all we had to do was give you money for the shears and you'd cut the golden fleece. *(He opens a letter)* Do you know what Papa wrote to me? "I was counting on René, who has sent me nothing. Is he going to let our bank, that was held up with so much effort, tumble down? If the creditors put my back against the wall, they'll take me to court."

(RENÉ crouches on the sofa, picks up his flask listlessly)

RENÉ. Papa's been using the bank to loan himself money. That's why his bank is in trouble.

EDGAR. Fine. Even if I sell a painting a week I can't make enough to stop them from—

RENÉ. American-style business wiped Papa out. I worked hard as the family executor.

EDGAR. For which you charged us substantial fees. God, we can't talk with you without getting billed. *(Confronting him with the charges)* Look at this: conversations with Michel Musson, your own uncle, whose house you live in *gratis*, ten hours. And this, bank deposits for Uncle, conversations with Didi, Mathilde, and Tell Musson. My God, you even billed us for talking to your own wife.

RENÉ. But I charged you a reduced fee.

EDGAR. You knew the cotton business was failing and you gouged funds. You were my favorite brother. God, I trusted you. You had it all, and you took it all.

RENÉ. I am appalled you think I would do anything unethical. The authorization for my action was Papa's idea. In reference to your...accusation...about my charges. I and my assistants have spent many hours working...You have benefited...directly from the money you have received...your gallery openings, your studies, your trips as well as indirectly from Mama and Papa's generosity to you from monies they've received. It's not my fault the cotton business is failing. *(He pushes* **EDGAR** *violently into a chair)* If you chastised me for my liaison with Mrs. Olivier, that I could understand. I feel guilty about that.

EDGAR. What... are you saying? You are...sleeping with America? You're not... You are. Here?

RENÉ. She understands me. Comforts me.

EDGAR. Your baby is dying, your wife is critically ill, and you're having an affair with her neighbor in her house?

RENÉ. It didn't just start now.

EDGAR. When did it start?

RENÉ. A year ago.

EDGAR. I practically gave Tell to you. You couldn't tell me about America all these months I've been here. We all have to deal with unbearable situations. But we don't bring our mistresses into our house.

RENÉ. I hate myself. But God, I am bored. There's no defending it. I've become the men I knew. I wake up and see, like Papa and Uncle, I've a mistress and a wife. I want it to end, but it's impossible. I'm too exhausted. Too disappointed. When we're alone, America's different. She lifts my spirits. *(Pause)* No one believes in monogamy anymore. We only choose it when we have no appealing alternatives. *(Goes to the window, looks out.)* Sex is everywhere in this city, except in a husband's relationship with his wife. I say I love my wife, but I'm cold below the neck. I feel nothing. She's attractive to many men, but to me she's not, so I wear a mask. Wives dream of other husbands, husbands dream of other wives, and we both shut our eyes.

EDGAR. Does Tell know about America?

RENÉ. *(Awkwardly)* I guess she suspects. I don't want to lie, so I'm evasive. It takes so much energy. Believe me, being a liar is tiring.

EDGAR. *(Clumsily, scared of what he is going to say)* People don't talk about falling out of love even if it has a happy ending. When I came here, I wanted to die but *(Fearful)*–Your wife tempted me back... So. The angriest I can get at you is a neutral stance because...you and I are the same sorts...We would like to keep happy with the old and new ways because there are benefits in both...I'm still in love--

RENÉ. Quiet. It's not life as usual. Right now I'm emotionally raw. *(Pause.* **RENÉ** *covers his face.)*

EDGAR. I'm still in love with your wife... When I lost her, I lost sweetness in my life. If you don't love her, *(Pause)* can I take her home with me?

RENÉ. Don't crowd me.

EDGAR. I'm letting you know how I feel. *(*RENÉ *starts to cry. He moves apart.)*

RENÉ. You would need my written permission to board the ship.

EDGAR. You could have the children...if you want them.

RENÉ. *(Chuckles painfully)* I like them better this month than last.

EDGAR. I understand your life isn't settled and the odds of Tell and I getting together are messy--

RENÉ. Take her... But do it quick.

(blackout)

Scene Two

(A week later. **EDGAR**, **TELL** *and* **EMILY** *walk cautiously down an alley.* **TELL** *pauses, a look of growing uneasiness comes over her face)*

(A banjo twangs and several musicians, hidden in an archway, rasp out, "Oh Susannah, oh don't you cry for me.")

EDGAR. Let's set a deadline for our departure. Two weeks?

MUSICIAN. *(offstage)* Move on.

EDGAR. I've been telegraphing France. René's gone through all the money. Your father's, my father's, the family banks.

TELL. Let's talk later.

EDGAR. When I get back, I'll have to do dozens of pastels to save the family. I can't come back for you. Little Jo wants to go with me.

TELL. You asked her? Wouldn't a wife and four children kill your art? You couldn't paint eighteen-hour days.

EDGAR. I want to comfort you, and take you out of this pain.

TELL. You can't. Little Jeanne is so weak. Now baby Odile has a fever. Jo's relatives wouldn't let her leave the country.

EDGAR. This city is dangerous! You and I tried to make it work. Did all we could to force New Orleans to be reborn. The universe has its own plans...I will protect you in Europe...Yes, I'm free, but I need grounding. When I'm alone, I work for hours, forget what day it is, lose connection to family and friends. With you— even with children screaming, we'd move into a deeper reality, a closeness. I can't go back to living alone. I'll paint. Sell my paintings. You'll have confidence in me, and I'll go and get famous and get you more and more help. Now is the lowest point we'll have to face. Oh, don't refuse me. I'm asking you to come with me to Paris. Choose yourself. Choose me.

TELL. If I go away, I'll never see my children again. René's—not the person you knew. He's confused. Be careful of the homeless by that Church. Speak in English and low.

(SOUND: *Man offstage yells: "Stranger, get out.")*

*(*EMILY *appears suddenly from around a corner with* **NORBERT***.)*

EMILY. Are you and Tell coming with us?

EDGAR. My trunk is packed.

TELL. Mine too.

EMILY. Norbert thinks he can get Tell a holiday pass. Otherwise they may not let her on board. Even with René's written permission. Without her French husband some may not want her to leave the country.

EDGAR. But if she leaves on vacation with relatives via Havana on a French ship?

TELL. And with a large crowd of people. Other women and children.

EMILY. She can make it to Paris like I'm going to do next week and never come back.

TELL. I thought you were leaving in two months?

EMILY. We have been warned to leave at once.

TELL. I don't know if my children can go. My husband may not let them—

EDGAR. Tell needs more time.

TELL. Can't you wait a few weeks. It would be so much easier to travel with others—

EMILY. We can't! To stay, we have to register with the authorities and get the protection of a white patron. Norbert would like to...but no one will honor him—

(Noises of men shouting, a gunshot.)

EDGAR. Where is the watchman who is supposed to patrol?

(More sounds of a skirmish)

EMILY. Take your luggage and get out. Before they send a pack of dogs and madmen to get you.

(Two soldiers barrel toward them, as if they would knock them down.)

TELL. Oh...no.

EDGAR. Get back!

EMILY. Shush. We don't want a fight! *(She throws her arms in the air and rushes off)* God bless you. Goodbye.

(Music and slide in as she is leaving)

Scene Three

*(A few days later at the house. **TELL** sits on the porch. She has fallen deep into herself and finds relief for an instant in silence. **JO** comes in, dressed in a traveling cape and bonnet. With forced gladness, she taps her mother on the shoulder. **TELL** hugs **JO** to her breast..)*

JO. I'm ready.

TELL. Your whole life you have been with me. Now, different cities, different houses.

JO. I'll come back for the Carnival balls.

TELL. And Papa will present you. I can't take it.

JO. Don't cry, Mama, I'm not afraid anymore. I want to leave.

TELL. No, do you really?

JO. I'm grown up. *(She pauses—then speaks in a flat, empty tone)* I can travel alone. I'm leaving all my puppets. I placed them in a row for little Jeanne so she can play with them when she gets better. I'm too old for puppets.

TELL. Well, won't you miss them?

JO. I packed a baby one in my bag, but don't tell anyone.

TELL. *(Smiles as if she hasn't heard it)* I won't. Are you sure you want to go, you don't have to if—

JO. Don't stop me. Papa's folks need me. They won't let me leave the country.

TELL. Oh, I can't stand it. I shouldn't have told René you wanted to go to Paris.

JO. I want your life to be easier, Mama, you worry so. Trying to make everyone happy. I know how hard it is, because I see.

TELL. Oh, shush. I just need another hug.

(JO climbs on her lap, hides her face in her mother's shoulder)

JO. I'm only going for a while. Then I'll be at the convent in Mobile. I'll come back a grown-up elegant lady. Everyone will like me. Now I just make trouble for you.

TELL. *(Her voice shifting far away)* How can not having you be better for me?

JO. You'll see. Things will be easier.

TELL. Don't talk that way.

*(***DIDI*** *walks in from the front hallway, sits tensely on the sofa.)*

JO. There are too many people here. When people are squished like that it's hard for everyone to be nice. It'll be better for you if I leave. Even in New Orleans.

TELL. *(Rocking her like a baby)* You don't know, you don't.

JO. *(Curling a finger through* **TELL***'s hair)* Don't feel sad. I'm happy, Mama.

*(***MATHILDE*** *walks in briskly from the rear hallway. She looks at* **DIDI** *matter-of-factly)*

MATHILDE. You're in one of your depressive moods.

DIDI. Jo's been mine since she was three weeks old.

MATHILDE. I thought you were fine with her going.

DIDI. I've enough other reasons to be bitter and sad.

MATHILDE. Oh, yes. Edgar is also leaving.

DIDI. Don't talk. I don't want to fall apart.

(Reluctantly, **JO** *leaves her mother and walks slowly to where her aunts stand waiting)*

DIDI. *(To* **MATHILDE***)* I won't survive this.

MATHILDE. I didn't think I'd survive the death of my baby boy. I made it, and you will too.

(JO *feels her aunts' sad eyes on her and forces a smile)*

JO. I would like to say goodbye to you, Tante Didi and Tante Mathilde.

DIDI. Oh, no.

(UNCLE MICHEL *comes in from the back hallway—summoning his soldier's heartiness. Takes* JO *and gives her a pony back ride on his knee. He clicks his heels and waves an imaginary whip)*

UNCLE MICHEL. I'm proud of you, Jo. I'm glad your grandmother didn't live to see this day. I'll go with Jo. Soon we'll be galloping on horses on Pass Christian.

JO. You're too old, Grandpa.

UNCLE MICHEL. I never do things like old people. I feel like I'm three. I used to look around, and I was the youngest in the room, and now I'm the oldest. *(Another forced laugh)* I should leave also. After the fall of New Orleans, I refused to take the oath of allegiance to the Union, so they're not going to tell me what to do.

MATHILDe. You'd only get in the way, Papa.

UNCLE MICHEL. Jefferson Davis is writing a chronicle of the war. Now Jo's going, I can tell you for the past ten years I've been—

DIDI. Keeping a journal, we know.

UNCLE MICHEL. But Jo doesn't know the extent of the collection. I've been writing down each dream I've had along with every daily event and political occurrence. About fifteen hundred pages a year. For my heirs so they can know everything about me.

JO. About me too?

UNCLE MICHEL. Yes, I'm showing how the dream relates to the event and the routine. *(Tries to get his appeal started)* Well, what do y'all think? I've thousands of entries. Mr. Davis will find them interesting.

DIDI. Papa, she doesn't understand.

JO. Yes, I do!

MATHILDE. Shush. *(MATHILDE shrugs her shoulders and embraces JO)* You're such a big girl, so grown up, and you'll be even more so when you return from your Papa's people.

JO. I want to go with Uncle Edgar.

MATHILDE. Will and I are moving to Ocean Springs—that's not far from you. I'll visit. I'm only sorry Aunt Didi won't be with us.

DIDI. Thank God I don't have to cope with Will anymore.

UNCLE MICHEL. One more hug. René can't make you go if I say no.

JO. Don't worry about me, Grandpa.

MATHILDE. Don't blame René, we all agreed.

UNCLE MICHEL. *(Growls)* I never.

DIDI. Papa, please.

UNCLE MICHEL. Write me like you promised. A page a day.

JO. Yes, sir. Have Uncle Edgar send me a little sketch of the family.

MATHILDE. I almost forgot the lunch basket.

UNCLE MICHEL. We'll wait for you outside, Jo.

(UNCLE MICHEL smiles, blows his nose and goes out to the gallery. MATHILDE and DIDI give way to a flurry of guilty business and leave swiftly. While JO is bravely silent, EDGAR enters.)

EDGAR. Where's the little lady? I have a gift for you.

JO. A miniature of Mama! Oh, she's so beautiful. Thanks, Uncle Edgar *(Her face lighting up, JO kisses him gratefully)* Come with me to Mississippi. How will I learn to draw if you don't teach me?

EDGAR. Take my memorandum book.

JO. I couldn't.

EDGAR. All my life I've carried a notebook where I sketch images. *(Gives her a shiny binder)* I took this one when boarding the Scotia, the last paddle steamer. See, I've sketches of the passengers. Here I've drawings of horses, a genre painting called "Pouting," and the "Orchestra of the Opera."

JO. I couldn't draw like that. I dance even in my dreams, but if I try to draw—

EDGAR. Neither could I at first.

(She laughs and he laughs with her)

EDGAR. Study and paint, then come to Paris. I'll get you permission to copy inside the Louvre.

JO. *(She opens the book)* Let me sign my name. Jo Balfour 1873. *(Reluctantly)* Must we go?

EDGAR. Sometimes we must.

JO. I don't want anyone to know about the miniature. They might take it.

EDGAR. *(He looks at her with understanding sympathy)* It's our secret.

(SOUND: Music fades in slowly)

(EDGAR takes JO's hand and they walk out bravely to the gallery. She smiles, controlling an impulse to cry, clutching the miniature. MATHILDE comes out to the gallery—uneasily—with a plate of sandwiches. All feign smiles and hug JO with elaborately casual airs and pathetic attempts at heartiness. TELL hugs her to herself—sobs brokenly.)

(JO leaves slowly and her mother rushes back inside, bumping into RENÉ. Huskily trying to force a smile, RENÉ walks on to the gallery just as JO passes out of sight. He waves feebly. Mournful sounds of a carriage are heard. Moments later, AMERICA marches out. She attempts to catch RENÉ's eye, but he walks back inside, staring at the floor. There is a dead silence. AMERICA follows him inside with guilty talkativeness.)

AMERICA. Jo should have appreciated me more. She forgot to thank me. The girl's all right as people go, but one more child or less, in this house... what does it matter?

(MATHILDE and DIDI walk dully into the parlor. MATHILDE attempts a light, amused tone, and passes sandwiches. RENÉ loiters at the desk with AMERICA)

MATHILDE. These sandwiches look lovely on Mama's calendar plates with Monarch butterflies and roses.

DIDI. How can you talk of food when Jo's leaving?

MATHILDE. *(With understanding)* Edgar's going too.

(AMERICA glares at the sisters. Her face is stony and her tone icy)

AMERICA. Food shouldn't be eaten in the parlor. You want rats? Yesterday I saw one leap from the banana tree. We'll have to shave it back, replace that rosebush with a cement slab. We must economize if René's going to get back to Paris. Isn't that right, René?

(He doesn't respond and she leaves noisily through the pantry)

MATHILDE. People usually behave better with food.

(EDGAR enters, sees TELL and moves her to the side.)

EDGAR. Bad news on bad. I've just gotten a wire from my father. They've seized all his possessions. I will have to use every penny to release him.

(TELL moves away covering her face)

EDGAR. It won't always be this way...But I'll have very little time for you or anything at first when I get back. I'll have to paint one pastel after another and sell them to raise funds. Soon as we've money and you're divorced and remarried, I'll see that Jo joins us in Paris.

(She starts to cry.)

EDGAR. Here. Come. Shush. Once I'm successful, it will be like it was before the War. *(He blots her cheeks with a handkerchief)* I promise fidelity. *(Kisses her hand)* I want you to be my wife. Isn't that enough for now?

(TELL and EDGAR exit to the garden)

DIDI. *(Gloomily to MATHILDE)* When exactly are you leaving?

(MATHILDE pauses—then lowers her voice to a tone of whispered confidence)

MATHILDE. After Will's meeting at noon. I'm not sure where he went.

(We see a duel pantomimed on another side of the stage. **MATHILDE** *and the family members don't see or hear it.)*

MATHILDE. Excuse me if I gloat. I woke up this morning and thought, "Praise God I'm finally leaving." I'll have my own big house and my own room, thick sheets and a satin quilt. Aren't you happy for me?

DIDI. *(Her hopes dashed)* Yes...no. If only I could win a proposal.

(A shout offstage, "Fire on the one.")

DIDI. I should be happy for you, but I'm not. Abandoning me with Tell and Papa. He won't come in and she won't come out. *(Valiant)* Don't you need someone to read to the children?

*(The countdown begins as Dueler 1 (***MAN #1***) and Dueler 2 (***MAN #2***) pace. Offstage counter shouts, "Five.")*

MATHILDE. We'll get a nurse in Ocean Springs.

(Offstage counter screams, "Four.")

(The front parlor doorway opens and **UNCLE MICHEL** *walks in, with a quick glance at* **RENÉ.** *Children's voices are heard and* **UNCLE MICHEL** *confronts* **MATHILDE.)***

(Offstage counter screams, "Three.")

UNCLE MICHEL. Mathilde, little Will needs you. He's bawling for Edgar.

(Offstage counter screams, "Two.")

MATHILDE. Thanks, Papa.

(Vaguely resentful, **MATHILDE** *goes out.* **UNCLE MICHEL** *moves over to* **RENÉ**—*irritably)*

UNCLE MICHEL. It should be over by now.

(Offstage counter screams, "One.")

DIDI. *(Looks about, tense)* I have a feeling something bad's happened. What is it?

(Gunshots.)

RENÉ. Will's been in a duel.

(WILL collapses)

DIDI. What?

(The other dueler rushes over to WILL.)

(RENÉ pats DIDI's shoulder. She gives him an uneasy, almost frightened glance.)

(WILL gets carried offstage. Lights fade. End of duel sequence.)

UNCLE MICHEL. Will was set on a challenge. They were shooting pistols at noon. Strange, since it's usually dawn.

DIDI. We should warn Mathilde.

UNCLE MICHEL. It's over by now. Anyway, it's not women's business.

DIDI. We should do something.

RENÉ. Calm down.

DIDI. But Papa—

(AMERICA comes in from the pantry. She is terribly annoyed. She frowns at them suspiciously)

AMERICA. Are you talking about me again? Every time I leave and return I see these caught faces. The devil's going to punish you for talking about me. I won't have it.

RENÉ. We were discussing politics. A certain weariness in people getting their dream—

AMERICA. I know what I hear.

UNCLE MICHEL. *(To* **RENÉ***)* She'd be a good woman if someone held a gun to her head twenty-four hours a day.

AMERICA. How dare you—

UNCLE MICHEL. I'll do what I want. I'm the head of this house. And the head doesn't take orders from the tail. *(He takes a threatening step toward her, raising his cane)* Leave! I'm in a fighting mood. If I kill someone it might as well be you. Nobody would miss you.

(He goes out the front parlor—roughly—grazing past **MATHILDE***, who is coming back in. Her hands drop distractedly to her dress)*

MATHILDE. Somehow I'm so nervous today. We're all packed, Will has to run off. I don't get it. If he knows we're leaving, couldn't he stay home? What could be so important? *(With forced casualness)* Sweet Jesus, don't let him get into trouble.

*(***AMERICA*** comes in through the front parlor, goes straight up to* **MATHILDE** *and jeers.)*

AMERICA. It's such a disgrace. I just received word at the door, Will's been shot in a duel.

MATHILDE. Is he dead?

AMERICA. Wounded, slightly.

MATHILDE. Will's always tilting against windmills.

AMERICA. This time he killed a police officer.

MATHILDE. He...did...what?

AMERICA. They've posted a bond and thrown him in jail. You'll have to use your travel funds to bail him out.

MATHILDE. Well, get my hat and coat!

(Her reaction has an automatic quality as if it did not penetrate to real emotion. Her face darkens—stung, and she goes out. With a scornful shrug, **AMERICA** *cries)*

AMERICA. Don't bring Will in the front door! We'll never outlive the humiliation. *(She starts at* **RENÉ***)* If you're curious about what you can do to help out, I've got some suggestions...Are you listening to me?

RENÉ. I'm trying not to.

*(***RENÉ*** takes out his flask and drinks.* **AMERICA** *gives him a quick biting look and disappears through the back parlor. Moments later,* **EDGAR** *returns, suitcase in hand.)*

RENÉ. I can't believe you're leaving when we have so much trouble.

EDGAR. It's better for everybody if I go.

RENÉ. Better for whom?

EDGAR. For me and Tell.

RENÉ. What about me? I need you. I'm drowning here.

EDGAR. Talk to America.

RENÉ. Oh, don't give up on me. Stay. How could it be better with you miles away? *(With a cynically appraising glance)* So you are taking Tell to Paris.

EDGAR. *(Guiltily)* No...Yes. If she will go—

*(***UNCLE MICHEL** *comes in hastily from the back parlor. Goes worriedly to* **EDGAR***)*

UNCLE MICHAEL. This house is always in the middle of disaster. Now I have to get Will out of jail. *(A smile crosses his face as he hands* **EDGAR** *a magazine)* Something to amuse you on the ship. I think it's a sin to read these burlesque magazines. I read them anyway. So what. The problem with heaven is some awful people are going to be there so I'd just as soon be in hell.

EDGAR. Well...Thanks...Uncle Michel.

UNCLE MICHEL. It bothers my ears to hear my name. Before I was Michel Musson. That meant something. Now I don't know who I was five minutes ago, let alone next week. I'm sixty and I don't know who I am anymore.

EDGAR. The whole world is changing. People want to breathe freely...

UNCLE MICHEL. I don't understand your ideas about a New World. I want my old one back. My God, can't you stay? Your brother needs you. You're the strong one. Money was what you came here for, wasn't it?

(EDGAR looks away, shrinking into himself)

UNCLE MICHEL. You and René, prospecting in the New World. Take this for your trip.

(He pulls out a small roll of bills carefully selects one. **EDGAR** *refuses it)*

EDGAR. I'm fine.

UNCLE MICHEL. I'd liked to have given you more. Twenty years ago, I could have. It was a damn comfortable life. I hoped we'd have something in common... that you'd take an interest in the White League.

EDGAR. Oppressing the Negroes cannot be justified.

UNCLE MICHAEL. Everyone oppresses someone! Right, René?

(RENÉ shrinks in the doorway, **EDGAR** *stares at his watch without seeing it)*

UNCLE MICHEL. I don't know what I did to offend you...I welcomed you into my home. I treated you like the son I never had. *(Calls distractedly to* **RENÉ***)* René, we have a meeting to attend.

(RENÉ shrugs guiltily, and skulks out the rear parlor door after his uncle. **DIDI** *enters, breathless from the gallery, spots* **EDGAR***.)*

DIDI. So, you're leaving. Can't you wait till summer? You haven't experienced anything till you've spent a day out in the boiling air and open sun. It's really refreshing. The heat just hangs there between the oak trees. I picked you a boutonniere. *(She pulls out a flower she's been hiding behind her skirt, touches his lapel. He draws away, smiling uncomfortably.)*

EDGAR. I'll do it.

DIDI. Mama used to have a flower lady who came every week and taught me what to do. Hold still a minute.

EDGAR. I don't know if I can. *(Hesitates)* They like you to board early...Where did I put the ticket?

DIDI. Your jacket? Check the front pocket. Where? Oh.

EDGAR. I hope I didn't pack it.

DIDI. There it is.

EDGAR. You're so observant.

DIDI. That's what you said when I first visited Italy. You said I found more subtleties in your painting than anyone. Because I saw the suffering.

(DIDI gives a quick suspicious glance to the entranceways, then kisses him passionately. He backs off and turns her away from him.)

EDGAR. Forgive me if I've done anything to mislead you. You're like a sister to me.

(She stiffens and backs out onto the gallery. Moments later, TELL comes in cautiously through the rear parlor doors.)

TELL. Edgar, are we alone? Good. I want to remember that feeling.

EDGAR. I've said little in lots of time. Now I feel I must say lots in little time.

TELL. All this time I saw myself going with you, but now—I don't know.

EDGAR. *(He walks her to the sofa, regarding her from somewhere far within himself)* There were a lot of things I didn't know. The brutality of your sun. Before I go to sleep I imagine you beside me, your body caressed by thick sheets, the quick-silver light falling on your thigh. Join me, Tell.

TELL. You're dancing with something bigger than me: your talent.

EDGAR. I'm wistful for a wife of my own.

TELL. René would never get over it. I know he has agreed but—

EDGAR. He will have America.

TELL. Three children and a blind wife.

EDGAR. Finally, a family.

(She gives a forlorn toss of her head)

(SOUND: Carriage bells sound in the street. Offstage **TELL***'s baby lets out a harsh cough, another wails.)*

EDGAR. But we shouldn't take the children, now. They're too sick—

TELL. Well, I can't leave them. I've already lost Jo.

EDGAR. Although René agreed, he's now concerned—

TELL. You fear the children would distract you. You want to devote yourself to painting, after all.

EDGAR. Your baby has a hacking cough. Neither child is well.

TELL. How can I let my children believe their mother abandoned them?

EDGAR. Only for a short while.

TELL. Where's René?

EDGAR. He went for a walk.

TELL. *(Sobbing)* I don't want to stop loving you.

EDGAR. You won't. I know now, I am not a New Orleanian, a Southerner, an American. I am almost a son of Louisiana but I am completely a painter from France. I am French, and you can be that too. By living in Paris.

(Rain falls outside.)

EDGAR. I will send René money when I can and I'll pay for you to visit New Orleans, but I'm never coming back. Your vision and mine will only get worse here.

(It begins to rain as if the town were crying. She paces going for her suitcase then putting it back.)

TELL. Leave quick. Pour all your thoughts into images, so people will remember New Orleans and see me the way you did when we were together. *(She touches his lips.)* Go, before we...

EDGAR. Do something impulsive: jump the fence, strip naked, swim the Mississippi. I want you now, today.

(SOUND: Bell chimes)

EDGAR. Run off with me. Leave. My best art was done like that, in a flash. A release of spirit, a concession to a greater power.

TELL. If I went... your paintings would suffer.

EDGAR. But my heart would grow. I have to step back and take care of bigger things than my painting, things that painting didn't take care of. There is an illusion that art can save us. Dreams do not go away. They go to the grave with you. Sometimes as you move toward a dream, the dream meets you.

(SOUND: Carriage bells)

EDGAR. Well, it's time for me to go.

TELL. No, no, no.

(He touches her face and she his forehead, eyes, mouth. She buries her face in his neck. He draws her away, but she gets up and throws her arms around him—)

EDGAR. I don't think we were meant never to see each other. I don't think I was never meant to hear your voice or the ripple of your laugh.

TELL. Don't forget me.

(EDGAR breaks away and leaves quickly out the front parlor door. Her hands flutter to her eyes to wipe back the tears. Her two sisters join her, coming in hastily from the rear parlor. The three cousins rush to the gallery window to wave farewell. DIDI, forcing a laugh, inches in front and waves the most. RENÉ walks in from the pantry. He goes somberly to the window. Once EDGAR has gone, RENÉ steps back into the parlor and busies himself at the desk and speaks with a sad bitterness to TELL, who comes into the parlor.)

RENÉ. Tell, I wish there were something I could say. *(Pause)* I won't ask any questions and you shouldn't ask any questions. Maybe this way we can live together.

TELL. I hope so.

(MATHILDE comes in and walks TELL to the gallery. MATHILDE sits on the arm of TELL's chair, her arm around her. DIDI joins them, standing behind TELL's chair)

DIDI. He's gone.

TELL. Paris took him back. I wonder if anyone will know that Edgar came to New Orleans?

(Music plays softly)

Epilogue

(EDGAR walks slowly to the ship's railing. He peers out, a far-off quality in his voice)

EDGAR. I stand on the deck watching New Orleans fade into light. It feels like peering through a looking glass, hallucinatory, the vast wild sky expanding into mirror-like water. I'd come to find the people to whom I belonged—to close up this hole in my soul.

No, I'd come for Tell, If only I'd captured her beauty in my painting. On board, I paint her drenched in rain light in a white long gown with hundreds of brilliants. Her skin shimmers with brightness. I paint her home on Esplanade, the half-exposed bodies, caught up in light and shade, bare shiny arms with a vaguely underwater feeling, the wonderful warmness and profanity of life. I paint the overall view of them, shapes of light and shadow brushing their faces. Rain—inside and out, behind their eyes, inside the brush as I weave their forms on the canvas.

(Terrified, he speaks, and the characters drift onstage in a final tableau)

Water rolls by, great stretches of ocean, and rain falls, inside and out, and I leave New Orleans, and my relatives. Uncle Michel, Little Jo, Didi, Mathilde, and Tell. Sweet beautiful Tell. I let them face into the ocean. Watery wind, fog, nothing can stop me from painting. I see their outstretched arms in the foam. Their hurting gray faces in the mist.

Raw emotion bleeds through. And Edgar the artist is back, painting with a new ambition. For the glory. For the precision. For the defiance of death. And as memory fades I capture one impression and then another. It's all I can do. Light takes hold and color. I keep painting. Silver, blue, gold, and lavender. I immortalize my family in this new painting, I call "Impressionism." For nothing is permanent.

I bite my lip and keep working till Paris is in view. I recall Hannibal's words in crossing the Alps: "We will either find a path or make one!"

(He continues sketching, 3 slides appear in incandescent rainbow colors, ending with something like "The Portrait of Estelle.")

(JO dances in, her ballet movements filling the stage. She twirls bravely, with a voracious delicacy reminding us of Degas' "Fille de Quatorze Ans." There is an uncanny, gay freedom in her manner as if in spirit she were released to live again.)

(Curtain)